Alex
Hated the Morning . . .

The headache nudged her gently at first, almost politely, from a distance: sorry, old pal, here I come again, it's wake-up time. As the familiar throbbing began to turn into something that wouldn't be ignored, Alex tried covering her head with the pillow. It was a flimsy, nothing pillow, no defense at all against the assaults of another day. A no-good pillow, not her own. Who the hell's pillow was it . . . ?

Bleary-eyed, she started a tentative look around. Some kind of loft, sparsely furnished. There was someone else in the bed with her. She could see the back of a man's head, well-groomed hair, dark with highlights, expensively cut. And his shoulders—wearing a shirt? A little odd. Suddenly she felt chilled, despite the bright sun that glared at her through sheer curtains. She pulled the sheet up around her shoulders. The sheet felt cold, too, cold and damp, and . . . sticky . . .

Her eyes opened completely and widely now, staring in horror at the deep red blood, still wet, that soaked the sheet.

The Morning After

A Novel by Eileen Lottman

Based on the Screenplay
by James Hicks

PUBLISHED BY POCKET BOOKS NEW YORK

This novel is a work of fiction. Names, characters, places and incidents are either the product of the author's imagination or are used fictitiously. Any resemblance to actual events or locales or persons, living or dead, is entirely coincidental.

Another *Original* publication of POCKET BOOKS

POCKET BOOKS, a division of Simon & Schuster, Inc.
1230 Avenue of the Americas, New York, N.Y. 10020

ISBN: 0-671-63570-0

First Pocket Books printing December, 1986

10 9 8 7 6 5 4 3 2 1

POCKET and colophon are registered trademarks
of Simon & Schuster, Inc.

Printed in the U.S.A.

The
Morning
After

Chapter One

THE HEADACHE NUDGED HER GENTLY AT FIRST, ALMOST politely, from a distance: sorry, old pal, here I come again, it's wake-up time. Alex tried to burrow deeper into the abyss, but the familiar throbbing began to turn into something that wouldn't be ignored: a rock beat, pound, pound, stomp and repeat, repeat, repeat the beat, the beat like an acetylene torch doing surgery on her skull. Light jumped mercilessly against her eyelids. She tried covering her head with the pillow but it was a flimsy, nothing pillow, no defense at all against the assaults of another day. A no-good pillow, not her own. Who the hell's pillow was it . . . never mind, try climbing back down into the blessed nowhere.

But the headache was getting rougher and the beat went on, and now someone was shouting at her insistently. The voice was vaguely familiar, male, falsely warm, authoritative, confident. A public

7

voice, talking to an audience: television. She woke more fully into the headache and dry mouth and queasy stomach of a major hangover, up against the incessant torture of the sound and light. Television was too hard to take in the morning; rock music and cheery-up voices had no business in anyone's bedroom.

And whose bedroom might this be? Oh, God . . . she almost never did this any more. She hated it. She was getting too old for waking up in a strange place to use someone else's toothbrush and make conversation. Her long, waved ash-blond hair fell like a soothing wall between her and the world, but its thickness couldn't hide her for long. The TV babble started to separate into bits of understandable English—an interview was going on against the beat of the goddamned music. In a minute she'd open her eyes.

Moans and sighs seemed to be emanating from the TV under the pulsing rock beat (would it be easier if it synched up with her headache? probably not) and she heard another man's voice gently grunting, "Good . . . that's good . . . gimme more, more . . . beautiful, oh yes . . . more of that . . ."

Good Lord, is this what they had on the early morning shows? Soft porn for early risers? She pushed back the pillow an inch or two and exposed one gray-green eye, smeary with mascara.

"You ever think about film, Bobby?" the interviewer asked, voice-over, with grunts and oh-yeahs going on all the while like an obscene Greek chorus.

"All the time," a voice replied cheerfully. Then it added—on what TV would call a more serious note—"How do you mean?"

Alex's eye opened ever so slightly against the brutal daylight and the shrieking-white screen where wild images tossed around with energy and abandon. Oiled, sleek young female bodies wore what looked like stickers but were either underwear or bikinis. They were grinning and gyrating under too-bright lights while a handsome young photographer leaped around and clicked off shots with one of his many cameras. While the interview was going on voice-over, film was running to show how agile the guy was, how eagerly the girls contorted themselves for him.

Alex's stomach seemed okay, quiescent for now, and the headache was probably as bad as it was going to get, at least until she stood up. Half of her couldn't help listening to the interview—it was too loud, too insistent. Her large gray-green eye, blood-shot and rimmed with last night's makeup, reflected the manic action on the screen. Bobby Marshack was the photographer's name; she had seen his photo in *People* or was it *New York* or *Vogue* or who cared.

"Y'think you'll graduate to films, the way Gordon Parks—"

As if he had too much energy to wait out the whole question, Marshack interrupted the inter-viewer with "Oh, sure, I've done a few."

"Were they released?"

Well, they'd done it, they'd finally forced her awake. Alex had both bleary eyes open now, and she started a tentative look around. She pushed her pale hair back off her face. Where the hell was this? Some kind of loft, sparsely furnished. The bed, start with the bed. She found herself naked, half-covered with a sheet. Slowly, respectful of the headache, she rose up on one elbow. The goddamned TV was still hammering at her. Bobby Marshack answered the interviewer's question to the accompaniment of more film showing himself shooting pictures of four or five models at once.

"The films I made were just for a few friends," he said in a deliberately suggestive voice.

Alex turned her attention away from the stupid and began to deal with reality. There was someone else in the bed with her. She could see the back of a man's head, well-groomed, dark with highlights, expensively cut. And his shoulders—wearing a shirt? A little odd. There she was bare-ass and there he was—*who?*

"But times are changing, Bobby," the interviewer said.

Suddenly she felt chilled, despite the bright sun that glared at her through sheer curtains. Another L.A. scorcher, but there was a breeze, and Alex felt suddenly cold. She pulled the sheet up around her shoulders. The sheet felt cold, too, cold and damp, and . . . sticky. . . . Her eyes opened completely and widely now, staring in horror at the deep red blood, still wet, that soaked the sheet.

"How do you mean, times are changing?" Bobby Marshack's insolent, easy voice asked her.

"You know, things are more permissive," the interviewer said.

Alex stared in disbelief at her right hand. It was all she could focus on. It was covered with dark, half-clotted blood. Her hand. Her blood? She sat up, unsteadily, and put one bare foot and then the other down on the cold floor. She was naked, and her almost too lean, long and beautiful body was unsteady on its pins, more than usual.

"You might do well," the interviewer said in his pseudo-thoughtful TV voice.

"I always do well," the photographer chuckled.

Alex looked around, tentatively. Where in hell was this? The sleeping area of a loft. There were sheer curtains on the window, tossing lightly in the breeze. Stark white walls, freshly painted, glaring. The room was empty except for a few packing crates, a couple of soft buttery leather chairs, a dresser, a large modern second-rate painting, the television set and, of course, the bed.

In a kind of shock, she found herself listening very attentively to the interview, as she got shakily to her feet and carefully took a step or two. Make sense of something, focus on the words.

"But y'don't understand. Movies, a moving picture, can't be as sexy as a still photograph." Alex nodded slowly, not agreeing with Marshack but testing whether her head would stay on as she made her way across the room.

"Why do you say that? They can film anything nowadays. Look at—"

No way was the subject of this publicity trip going to let the host hog the mike even for the time it took to end a sentence. "Think of a still photograph, a girl looking a certain way, lit a certain way. There's an angle . . . maybe the light and the angle's fixed, but the look . . ."

He trailed off suggestively. Alex looked. The girls were still gyrating, the asshole photographer was still snapping away in their midst, the rock music was still pounding and the voices over were still nattering. What the hell—was time standing still? Had the world gone all funny? Where the fuck was she and *who was that guy and where did all the blood come from?*

She picked up her dress from a heap on the floor, walked around the bed, past the man's feet. They protruded over the edge, wearing stylish black shoes.

". . . that only last maybe a 200th of a second. And there's no woman in the world can keep that . . . moment going. So they crank away, the porn kings, but it's all trash except that one 200th—and that's where I come in. I catch that split second permanently, y'hear what I'm saying?"

The music swelled up to overwhelm the voices as a signal that Bobby Marshack's time was up. Alex grabbed the man's shoulders to turn him over. She rolled him onto his back. His shirt was all red in front, unbuttoned. His chest had gashes in it, deep bloody holes. One of the holes had a kitchen knife sticking out of it.

Very slowly, she raised her eyes up to look at the dead man's face. Despite his frozen stare, he was easy to recognize. It was Bobby Marshack. She'd never seen him before in person, only just now on the television. Filmed, not live. She'd never seen him "live." She whirled to face him on the TV.

But the interview had been replaced by a garish commercial. Crazy Louie would undercut anybody's prices. Alex stared for a moment, wanting a replay, a different decision, madly wondering if there was a rewind button to make it all go by again, a little slower so she could make sense out of it, change it so

12

that it came out differently . . . in shock, she turned away from Crazy Louie to the man in the bed. His time on television was over, and so was his time in this world. He was *dead*. No rewind button for him . . .

"What're you trying to pull?" she asked him quietly, calmly. "Hey?" She wanted desperately to believe that this was some elaborate practical joke, even though she knew better. Still, maybe . . . oh, God, maybe . . .

"Is that one of those . . . ?" A trick knife? She looked more closely. It wasn't.

"Things haven't been bad enough?" she asked, still quiet, still calm, only to herself now.

She moved away from the bed, thoughtfully, trying to piece it together. Okay, where is this? What am I doing here? How long have I been here?

And then, after a long moment: Did I do this?

Chapter
Two

SOMETHING SOFT RUBBED AGAINST HER BARE LEG. HER mouth was too dry to scream. It was a little Siamese cat with huge hungry blue eyes. He cuddled gently against her as if for mutual comfort. The television went on bleating—local news, weather, commercials. Alex stood for a long time in the doorway of the bright sunlit room, all fresh white paint except for the fresh red blood on her hands and more, dried and darker, on her thigh where she must have brushed up against . . . him . . . in the night. She looked down at herself critically. Too thin, but still in the right proportions, no trace of California sun on her fair skin, polish on her fingers but not her toes, and no rings on her fingers or anywhere else. She was not in bad shape for a 42-year-old dame who'd been around the track a few times, but right now she would have traded this body, as is and where it is, for practically anyone else's anywhere in any shape. Alex was scared.

There was another room to this loft, just on the other side of the open door. It was dark and therefore inviting, but for a long time she couldn't move a muscle. The cat meowed inquisitively and she reached down to pet it, but stopped herself when she saw her hand, stained crimson, almost touching the smooth clean fur. She reached up to flip the lightswitch on the other side of the doorway.

It was your basic kitchen, clean, neat, well-equipped but nothing fancy. Alex went to the sink, turned on the water as hard as it would go, and stuck her hand under the tap. Blood swirled around the white porcelain and down the stainless steel drain; she tried not to think of the scene in "Psycho." When her hand was very clean she turned off the faucet and reached up to pull open the door of the cabinet directly overhead. Dishes, glasses. She tried another, and another, and found one that held the glue to put her back together: a stand of whiskey bottles. She chose a good Scotch.

The cat waited companionably while she poured and drank two quick shots. One of the cabinets had a few cans of food in it. With a steadier hand she took out a can of imported tuna. She opened it and set it down on the floor. The cat purred loudly and went for it. Alex went back into the bedroom, clutching the neck of the bottle, averting her eyes from the bed. She found her underwear and her purse, scooped them up and made her way to the bathroom. It was in semi-darkness, with just the spill of light from the doorway outlining the john, sink, tub.

She sat on the edge of the tub and took a long, heavy pull on the Scotch.

Her hands were still trembling as she dug into her purse for a cigarette and matches and, with some difficulty, managed to light up. Another shot of Scotch, a deep careful drag on the cigarette, and she started to feel real. Slowly, she got up, moved to the sink. After a minute she decided that she was not going to be sick. She filled the basin, took another deep breath, and plunged her face into the cold water. With one hand holding her damp hair away, she cooled the back of her neck with scoops of water, letting it run down her bare back and shoulders until she shuddered and stood straight. She reached for a towel—reasonably clean—and dried herself.

She reached for the switch, flicked it on. A row of bright lights framed the bathroom mirror. Alex studied her face without flinching.

She was still damned good looking, but every year of hard living showed. Her bleached hair needed work. Her eyes were puffed and swollen. She looked at herself without pity or censure; that was just the way it was. Not good, but enough to keep going a while yet. Her bones were indestructible, and the character lines so far only enhanced the high cheeks, wide-set eyes and firm chin. Her throat was starting to go; it would be a magnificent ruin soon if she didn't do something about it while there was still something to work with. Abruptly, she had too much of looking at herself. She switched off the lights. She dressed quickly in the pale light that fell across the white tile floor.

She had worn the blue silk dress last night.

Memory began, slowly, to return. She had been going to meet some important person that Jacky had lined up for her. At—what the hell was the name of the club? Martineau's. She remembered meeting someone, a woman, and not thinking much of her, making blotto with the vodka and then . . . nothing. She slipped the blue dress over her head and brushed through her long tangled hair with her fingers.

She had only scooped up one blue patent leather sandal—very high heels, she remembered putting them on last evening and thinking they made her legs look a little fuller in the calf, which was good—but she couldn't remember taking them off. She walked in the one high heel like a kid playing "born on the side of a hill"; that was a line Katharine Hepburn used in "Bringing Up Baby." It was funny then.

The blue-eyed cat came and waited for her in the doorway, licking its paws and whiskers contentedly. Dressed, Alex dug in her purse for her cosmetic bag. Apply a dab of eye-liner first thing. A bit of lipstick and a smidge of blush and your troubles might vanish just like that. She went back into the other room. She snapped off the television, which had moved on to a game show. She stood for a minute looking down at Bobby Marshack. No. She could not remember a goddamned thing, would have sworn she'd never seen the guy before in her life. Not in the flesh, anyway . . .

She shivered, cold. She shook her head—headache better now, almost gone—and walked over to the window. She held aside the sheer white curtain and looked out. Fierce sunlight, a dingy alleyway directly below, the street to one side, decrepit buildings, some abandoned, some boarded up. No traffic, no one around, even though it had to be well into mid-morning. Strange. She seemed to be on the second floor of the loft's building.

Alex strained her eyes against the glare to make out a distant street sign. Poinsettia? Or was it Palmetto? Palermo? She hadn't heard of any of the above but she knew damned well she wasn't in Beverly Hills or even Westwood. One of those downtown L.A. slums that every now and then someone thought they might gentrify with artists' lofts and a boutique or two to get things started. So far it hadn't worked, but what the hell, it might any day. She was here, wasn't she? She squinted into the shiny distance again but the street sign remained fuzzy.

She turned her back on the view and spotted her other shoe, upright on a high-tech chest of drawers. She went over to get it, and balanced on one foot to slip it on, while the blue-eyed cat snaked between her legs and purred loudly. Looking down at him, she saw that her knees had been scraped. She had no idea when, where, how. She was not unused to that sort of minor injury; like cigarette burns, one wakes up and finds them, that's all. No big deal. It happens to everybody, doesn't it? Doesn't everybody wake up to discover little damages and wonder . . .

A man's jacket hung across the back of a chair. Alex stared at it, reluctant to touch the dead man's things. She fought down a wave of nausea, the urge to run away. Desperately, she searched her memory for a glimpse of this jacket, a mental image of herself in this room, going to bed with this man—nothing.

18

She had no memory of anything after dressing, meeting some people at the restaurant, having a few drinks. Then nothing. Until she woke up to this horror.

The jacket might hold a clue. She took a deep breath and went over to it. She reached out her hand and touched the shoulder. It was just a blazer, lifeless, without the power to hurt her. She put her hand in the inside pocket, touched on a soft leather wallet. She pulled it out and turned it over in her hand: Mark Cross, expensive. She fanned out the credit cards and ID cards and driver's license, and checked the name over and over: Robert Marshack. The guy she'd just seen on television, alive and energetic and hard-selling himself, jumping around taking pictures, sharing his two-bit philosophy of life and art—she looked over at the television screen, but it was gray and flat and mute. She checked the money: not much. She replaced everything in the wallet and put it back in the jacket pocket. She checked the other pockets: nothing to tick off a memory of last night.

There was a white telephone on the floor at the foot of the bed. Being extremely careful not to brush against the crimson sheets—which were turning rusty as the blood dried—her back to the corpse, Alex picked up the phone, carried it to a straight chair, touching the number out as she walked. She sat down and listened as it rang twice and a machine said hello.

"This is Jacky. It's nine thirty and I'm on my way, but I'll be at the shop after—"

She hung up. Hesitating only a second, she began

tapping out another number. It rang once and was immediately picked up; Jacky started talking without bothering with preliminaries.

"Can it wait? I'm doin' this slalom over the canyon."

"I've got to talk to you," Alex said. She said it calmly, with controlled urgency. He didn't answer. *"Jacky?"* she exploded. The tension had been building inside her with inexorable force, and no place to blow off. She *needed* Jacky and he was treating her just like everybody else in his crummy world. Her hands were shaking out of control. She gripped the phone and tried not to go hysterical.

She could hear the wind whistling around him; he was driving with the top down. Probably one-handed, while he made the curves too fast and talked on the phone too slowly. "Right here," his voice came over finally, solid and strong. His slight accent lilted like a safety net swinging under her and Alex couldn't help a deep sigh of relief.

"What happened last night?" she asked him urgently. Her voice was low and tight in her throat.

Right away he got pissed off. "Christ, you start early! What're you boozin' for? Ten o'clock in the morning!"

"It's the Breakfast of Champions," she answered wearily. "Jacky, *please*. What happened?"

She listened to the sound of his wheels crunching gravel for a minute. "You fucked up again is what happened."

A wave of panic washed over her. "What d'you mean? How? I don't remember a damn thing!"

"You're really something, girl," Jacky said wearily. "You draw a blank whenever you . . ." He let it trail off. She listened to the wind, thought of the green trees along the canyon road. She waited for him to finish but apparently he wasn't going to bother.

"What did I do?" she demanded. She was desperate, surely he could hear that in her voice. Stop playing games with me, she was saying, I really need this information.

"Do?" he echoed. She waited, biting her lip, trying not to look at the dead man and all the blood. Jacky was deciding not to spare her; she knew him well enough to know when he was about to level with her for her own good. She lit a cigarette. "All right," he said at last. "I talked to a client of mine about you, a woman who could offer you the first reasonable gig you would have had in years. I told her how talented and beautiful, etcetera, etcetera, and she went all the way to Martineau's to find you."

He hesitated, or maybe he was just making a turn. Alex waited, her stomach starting to knot. "I couldn't be there to save your ass. I had business, but she goes herself," Jacky said. "And she calls me later to tell me she did like your style—or what's left of it—and then what do you do?"

He seemed to want an answer. "Why don't I remember any of this?" Alex groaned.

Jacky had a short laugh that could sound almost nasty. "You kidding me? You know what you did?" He couldn't see her answer, which was a slow shaking of her head, from side to side. "You called her a dyke. A greasy diesel dyke, to be exact."

Alex was really puzzled now. *That* wasn't her style. "What would I say that for?" she asked.

Jacky sighed. "Because she is one," he said. "But

you had to say it, didn't you? Now you're out and
I'm down a client. Thanks. And she was a steady
weekly regular, too. Short hair, no rollers, just a
good cut every ten days, no bleach and no kooky fad
styling, just a good cut that got around for people to
see, and now she's gone. Thanks."

"Listen, Jacky," Alex insisted. "Listen. I woke up
with a . . . a dead guy."

His reaction was not what she might have expected, or wished. Another unpleasant snort of
laughter. "You've got more serious problems than
lousy lovers, believe me," he said.

"I mean dead, Jacky. This man is cold."

She thought she heard the brakes as he slowed
down the Bentley. "You kidding me?"

"I'm looking at him."

"He had a heart attack?" Jacky asked carefully.

Alex almost smiled. "Yeah . . . from a knife in his
chest. And there's blood all over."

"Where are you? Home?" Before she could answer, he went on, talking fast now. "Wait, don't talk
on this kind of phone. Creeps listen in."

"What do I care? What do I *do?*"

"Shhh. Take it easy. Christ, Alex."

"Should I call the cops?" she asked him.

After a minute to think, he said, "I think you'd
better."

"But . . . I'm scared to, you know what I mean? I
mean . . . cops . . ." She waited, but he didn't answer. His silence scared her. "Jacky?"

"I'm thinkin', hon."

"Shouldn't I just get out of here?"

"You're still there?"

"Yeah. But I don't even know where—"

"Okay, okay, okay. It's bad if you run. You got to call the cops. And a lawyer. Hon, listen, we're gettin' a lot of static, the signal's tearing up, I'm going down into the canyon. Call me after you call the cops, all right?" She heard static and then he said, urgently, "I can't hear you. Alex?"

"Okay," she said, very quietly.

"Jesus," she heard Jacky breathe into the phone.

"I don't even know where I am," Alex shouted, panicked at the thought of losing him, even for a minute.

"Read the number off the phone. Tell the cops. They'll find you." A glob of static cut through, and then she heard him say, faintly, "It'll be okay, babe."

"You wanna bet?" she said. Jacky's phone clicked off. She sat there, listening to the dial tone, wishing with all her might she was sitting alongside him with the wind whipping through her hair and nothing to worry about except the next drink.

She took the phone toward the cool dark bathroom. The cat followed her.

What could cops think except that she must have done it? *She* wasn't so sure she hadn't—she just couldn't remember what she'd done instead.

She took her hairbrush from her purse and began brushing vigorously. Stimulated the brain—well, felt good, anyway. She poured a tumblerful of Scotch from the bottle and set it on the wide sink. After a few final strokes to her hair and a couple of hearty swigs at the drink, she examined the toothpaste, squeezed a bit on her finger and massaged her teeth. She straightened up and squinted at the mirror, and switched on the lights. She took another good, hard look at herself. She was trying to be objective, but it really didn't seem to her that this was the face of a murderer.

"You can go two ways," her drama teacher had told her. "Your face or your brain. You can go for the beauty pageants and become a movie star, or you can work hard and nurture your talent and become an actor." Althea had breathed the word "actor" as if it should be capitalized, like God. Naturally, every student at Northwestern had opted for the heavenly stage and the hard work, with starvation an odds-on probability. Well, nearly every student. Alexandra Sternbergen had sworn allegiance to the Bard along with all the other devout drama majors, but she was the one who was offered temptation. It was easy enough for them to stay pure—most of them had given it up to have babies or teaching jobs. A few played Shakespeare in the park, hoping for an occasional television commercial to pay the rent. But it had been Alexandra Sternbergen who got the apple dangled before her eyes, and she hadn't hesitated long before taking a big juicy bite.

Out of Paradise and straight to Hell . . . Hollywood treated her well, at first. The producer who lured her away from college before her senior year told the world she was the only actress in the world who could play Mary Queen of Scots as a great beauty, thus explaining Elizabeth's jealousy and the course of English history for the past four hundred years. He was an ass, and the script was pompous, but it had been a triumph for Viveca Van Loren. It won her rave reviews and a lot of money. She had never had money before. She sent a lot of it

24

home to her parents in Wilmette, and they were very proud of her.

She had changed her name with some kind of idiot notion that maybe Viveca could be a movie star and Alexandra Sternbergen would still be pure. She kept on thinking she'd work on the stage under her real name, maybe off-Broadway for no money, for her sins . . . but she never had the time. She made some good films, or so everybody said. She couldn't stand to watch them unless she had a few stiff drinks. One night she had gotten drunk and called her old teacher back at Northwestern, and Althea had been cold and not glad to hear from her. Alex had cried until she was drunk enough to pass out.

So she had taken Althea's advice, chosen between her face and her brain. She had chosen her face, and as she examined it in the stranger's bathroom mirror, she had to admit that she had probably made the right choice after all. Considering the spot she'd gotten herself in now, brains didn't seem to be her long suit. But the face was still good, damned good. They just weren't writing parts for her type right now; things were bound to change.

With something approximating self-assurance, Alex snapped off the light and returned to the bedroom. She looked at the body on the hideously crimson bed, at the dead television screen.

"Geronimo," she whispered softly, deciding. She petted the cat, popped on her sunglasses and walked the hell out of there.

Chapter
Three

———— · ———— · ————

NOTHING OUT IN THE HALL TRIGGERED ANY MEMORY OF having been there before. The floor was tiled and the lighting was shadowy; two or three blank doors led to other loft apartments, she supposed. There was no sign of life, no sound except her high heels rapping sharply against the old tiles as she hurried down the worn stairs.

Even with heavy-duty sunglasses, the day was blindingly bright and hot. The street was oddly silent. When she stepped outside, she looked up at the building. It was an old warehouse or factory, sandwiched between two vacant lots half-filled with trash and debris. A crumbling old stone archway over the door had the number carved into it: 544. A neighborhood in transition. The loft she had waked up in must hold many ancient ghosts as well as the considerably more recent one. Cut it out, Alex, and get back to your own turf where you can maybe start to think.

Shielding her throbbing head from the glare, she tried to look for a horizon, something peeking through the shimmering smog to give her a direction. A sharp glint of light—now you see it, now you don't—caught the sun like a distant signal: glass. High-rise buildings. This way to reality, or what passes for it. Resisting the urge to take off her shoes and run, Alex forced herself to take a slow look around first. She was in a very major jam and if she wanted to find her way out of it, maybe she'd better be able to find her way back here. She didn't feel like she'd killed anyone. She didn't know how someone felt after killing someone, but all she felt was a hangover. Wouldn't she feel guilty or something if . . . a residual drop of self-preservation instinct made her look around carefully for a street sign. She found one a block away, hanging askew on a corner post: Mateo. She groped in her purse for a pencil and a matchbook and wrote it down: 544 Mateo.

Trying not to stumble on broken sidewalks, she headed in the direction of the distant skyline. It had to be Century City. Bars and restaurants and shops and offices—civilization was there, beckoning like a mirage beyond the empty buildings and silent streets. Her heels clicked loudly, echoing like shots in the eerie landscape. Where the hell *was* everybody?

She picked her way carefully along littered and crumbling sidewalks for a couple of long blocks. Then, another mirage came into view—a yellow taxi, sitting against the curb alongside an intersection featuring a shuttered bodega, a burned-out building and two empty lots. She ran for it, grabbed the handle and yanked open the rear door. The driver looked up genially from his racing form.

"Laurel Street in Hollywood," she said, relaxing gratefully into the sprung leatherette cushions of the back seat.

The driver flipped the meter and started to roll. Graffiti and wall paintings and posters along the walls and fences made the barrio seem more colorful from the window of the cab than it had on foot. She leaned back and almost enjoyed it. One garage door had a huge multi-colored spray-painted head, quite realistically gross. The caption was in letters a foot high: DRAKULA ES NUMERO UNO.

Alex leaned forward. "What time is it?" she asked.

The driver glanced at the dashboard clock. "Ten fifteen."

"Friday," she guessed aloud.

"Thursday."

This exchange seemed to perk up his interest. He was trying to size her up, or meet her eye, in the rearview mirror, but she ignored him. He sounded amused as he went on, "November twenty-eighth." He paused, waited, craning to see her instead of watching the streets. "Nineteen eight—"

She cut off the gentle ridicule, just wasn't in the mood.

"Do me a favor," she said. "Stop by my bank. It's on the way."

The driver shook his head. "Won't do any good."

She glanced up sharply. He was smiling at her reflection. "November twenty-eighth," he repeated.

"So?" Alex said.

The driver shook his head in disbelief. "Turkey?" he tried to cue her. "Pilgrims and Indians and all that . . . ?"

"Shit," she answered.

"Is that a way to talk about a national holiday?"

"Then what're you working for?" she asked him.

"I thought you might need me," he said, grinning. He tried fixing the eye contact more solidly, but Alex was staring out the window. As you got to fancier neighborhoods in Los Angeles, the absence of human beings on the street became a normal and somehow comforting thing rather than a cause for alarm. The hibiscus and palms and increasingly green lawns as they headed west didn't register at all. There was something a bit more urgent on her mind, like the possibility of arrest, a murder trial, a room with no windows . . .

She couldn't think. She sure as hell couldn't think about *that*. She just had to concentrate on the next move. Clear her mind and make it a really smart move, for once. She stared down at her hands: ringless, slim, pale tapered fingers, shaking uncontrollably. Well-manicured, delicate but strong hands —were they capable of killing someone? Had it been self-defense? There wasn't anyone in the world who would believe that. Not this time.

"Hey, this inquiry about your bank?" the driver asked suddenly. "It's not your sweet way to beat me outa my fare, is it?"

Alex pulled a ten dollar bill out of her purse and held it up for him to see in the mirror. It shook a little. "Santa Monica and Fairfax," she said firmly. There, a decision. The driver was obviously impressed, she thought. Anyway, he kept his mouth shut for the rest of the trip.

Harry's Bar and Grill could not be mistaken for Harry's Bar in Venice, Rome, or New York. It was a good, solid, drinking-class bar with no pretensions. It was cool and dark and, at this time of the day, catered to solitary drinkers. When Alex entered, there were three men and an elderly woman already established on their stools at respectful but not unfriendly distances from each other. She sat down at the end of the bar.

Harry smiled in greeting. "Hey, Viveca! You were on again last night," he said. "Channel eleven. You're working your way down to the high channels." He poured her a shot of vodka and a tall seltzer with ice.

She sipped at the soda. "Harry, I forgot the bank. Could you cash a check?"

"Sure, Viv," he said.

She took out her checkbook and started writing. "Could you stand two hundred?"

"Ouch."

"I invited a whole gang out. You know, Thanksgiving." She gave him her semi-famous grin, full-blast.

"Ahh . . . okay," Harry nodded. " 'Best of the Yankees,' " he added.

"Pardon?"

"The picture last night," he said. "With Richard Egan . . . you were somethin', all right."

She took another drink of the seltzer. "I'm sorry I missed me," she said. She poured the vodka over the inch or so of water that was left on the ice.

Harry raised his own drink in a toast. "Here's to your tits, Viveca."

She downed the vodka. "Here's to your ass, Harry." She scooped up the ten twenties and walked out. A dire blast of brilliant sunlight slipped into the sanctuary before the door closed behind her.

She looked down at her hands on the steering wheel—steady now. Back in control. The light changed and she stepped on the clutch, which groaned in protest but allowed her to shift gears. 1963 was a good year for Mercedes, too bad it was so long ago. She drove with caution, out of respect for the uncontrolled substances she had already imbibed. I ought to eat something, she thought as she pulled past the Big Bob 24-hour supermarket, but the thought of food threatened the armed truce she had established with her stomach. She concentrated instead on the control she was exhibiting over the klutzy clutch as she snaked more or less gracefully into the driveway of her building.

It was on a good street, one of those rambling two-story apartment complexes that hide gardens and terraces inside unprepossessing brick facades. Her apartment was airy and fair sized for a one-bedroom, but she had never quite pulled it together. It was furnished in Early Impulse, faded or forgotten ideas of decor and style that never really went together. As Jacky had pointed out, the apartment lacked follow-through. The cheery chintz fabric on the oversized couch was supposed to be the focus of color for spinoffs—drapes and chair cushions and wallpaper were going to pick up key colors from the couch. But after nine years the walls were still painted boring white and the windows were un-draped and the Chinese rug didn't go with anything.

Alex crossed through the living room, and swore automatically under her breath at the oppressive heat. Kicking off her shoes and leaving them wher-ever they landed, she went into the bathroom, pulled open the medicine cabinet, and swallowed a few pills. Nothing heavy, just enough to get to the next move. As she started to close the cabinet, a thought struck her and she stood poised for a minute, to consider it. It only took a minute. She went into the bedroom, rummaged in the closet and came up with a traveling cosmetic case. She had left the medicine cabinet ajar; she reached up and swept all the prescription vials into the bag.

In the next few minutes, she moved faster than she had all day: get the suitcase down from the closet shelf, open it on the bed, toss the cosmetic case in it, then back to the closet to start pulling out clothes, no time to decide what, don't worry about which shoes, just the ones you grab, a belt, a bunch of underwear from a drawer—everything dumped into the case as the panic mounted.

She stripped off the blue silk dress and threw it in the closet to be bundled off to the cleaners one of these days. A long session in a jet shower helped her head. She put on a slim linen skirt with a bright silk blouse and jacket. She glanced at the suitcase, still messily open on her bed. She moved toward the telephone, but before she could get to it, it rang loudly, startling her.

Breathless, frozen in mid-gesture, Alex waited for it to stop. It took a very long time.

If she had moved quickly before, she now went

into frenzied action. She picked up the receiver and held it in her hand while with the other she ripped through the pages of the phone book to AIRLINES. She let the book slide while she punched out a number. She waited for several rings, then: "Thank you for calling AirCal. Due to holiday traffic all our reservation lines are busy. Please hold, you'll be—"

The fuck I will, she thought, pulling their plug. She glanced down at the yellow pages and hit another bunch of buttons.

"Thank you for calling Golden West. All our lines are busy at the moment but please—"

Alex slammed down the phone, hard. She grabbed the suitcase and ran from the apartment.

The sleek white Bentley eased into Jacky's space. He slid gracefully around and up from the driver's seat. Muscular and wide as he was, religiously regular workouts kept him lithe and agile. He had a broad, open face, with dark eyes that seemed to be laughing most of the time and a mouth that said "Trust me." Women liked Jacky and he loved them; they sensed that, which probably accounted as much for his success as his hairdressing skills.

Jacky reached over to the passenger side for the leather handle of the enormous wig box, and headed into the private side entrance of his salon. He owned the building, a two-story manor with a winding driveway in the front where chauffeurs could hand their ladies over to his care. The grounds were perfectly landscaped, and the gardener was there now, weeding, standing to salute respectfully as Jacky got out of his car.

Stepping into the salon, Jacky got his usual high

from the elegance of it. He loved it. It was beautiful, tasteful, chic, expensive. The reception area was inviting, with comfortable chairs discreetly arranged near the desk, and a modest display of Jacky's own line of hair care and health products blending in with the decor. He didn't look in the mirrors that reflected around the reception area—he didn't have to. Joaquin Manero had come a long way and was still on the move.

Red was reading a magazine behind the desk. All alone in the place, she hadn't even bothered to turn the music on. Jacky nodded to her and headed for the half-flight of stairs that led to the mezzanine, where he ministered to his own inner clientele, the elite, the rich and famous heads.

Red held up a handful of phone messages, flapping them to get his attention. Jacky stopped on the first step and walked back to the desk. "Viveca phone?" he asked, carefully casual.

"Nope," she answered. "Just these."

He took them. "Thanks for opening up, Red," he said. "Why don't you take off now. I just got a couple heads to do for parties."

As she reached for her purse, he said, "Make sure I get a line upstairs, will you?" Red nodded and did some fancy work with the state-of-the-art computer phone. Jacky was looking through the messages. "Miss Harding say what it was about?" he asked her.

"Nope."

"I hope nothing's going wrong with the party."

"Oh, you kidding? What could go wrong?" Red asked with a sigh. She was a transplanted New Yorker and her accent came out under the slightest emotion. This time it was clearly envy. "They got it down pat by now, every Thanksgiving they give the party, it's the biggest thing in town, maybe in the world. There'll be pictures of it in the papers tomorrow. Things wouldn't dare go wrong. Lucky . . ."

"Who, the Hardings?" Jacky asked idly.

"No, you," Red answered. She shrugged. "You go to this sensational mansion in Bel Air, and you go right in upstairs and you do her hair, then you get to stay, right?"

He didn't answer immediately. Red stabbed him with a curious glance, waiting for an answer. He nodded. "For a while," he said. He started upstairs with the wig box. "Thanks again for comin' in, Red. Have a good holiday."

"Yeah. You, too. Get your picture in the paper, you hear? It's terrific for business!"

Sometimes he thought he ought to replace her with someone more soignée, more thin and blond and maybe with an accent from one of those preppie schools out east, but Red was a good scout and loyal and—the most important thing—the clients liked her. Maybe she reminded some of them of the old days in Brooklyn.

By the time he reached the top of the winding stairs, Jacky had let Alex and her predicament fill his mind again. The truth was that she was never very far out of his thoughts these days.

Chapter Four

THE SAN DIEGO FREEWAY IS NOT WHERE YOU WANT TO be on a holiday when the thermometer is at 92 degrees Farenheit and you're driving a 1963 Mercedes that needs work. Alex leaned on the horn a lot; at least *that* still functioned. The traffic was hideous, and everyone was in a foul mood—why the hell weren't they all sitting around a big goddamned table and gorging themselves, it was goddamned un-American for all those goddamned cars to be out on the fucking freeway when she was trying to catch a plane. Didn't they care, didn't anyone give a goddamn for anyone any more . . . she was almost in tears. Self-pity, so that's how low you've sunk, Alex. Letting the heat and the traffic and the need for a drink get to you? And a goddamned murder . . .

She punched the horn, leaned her head on the

steering wheel for a second and then sat straight again, back in control. Close, but not bottoming out quite yet, thank you. Move your cars, Alex has got to get out of town. Rather urgently.

Running away? Is that what you're doing, Alex? You bet your ass.

She passed the cemetery where Al Jolson was buried, and Clauson and finally Sepulveda, turning off toward the airport. Local traffic, stops and starts. The Mercedes growled a couple of times but kept on moving. The airport itself was inner-lined with a huge horseshoe road, with little walkways booby-trapping you every few yards. She pulled to a sudden unscheduled stop as a family of four started to straggle unhurriedly across. Probably because her brake lights hadn't worked in a while, there was a deafening screech behind her and a hulking old Chevy—radiant in four shades of primer—just barely managed to avoid rear-ending her. The driver swerved and came up alongside, looked over at her curiously. At least he wasn't shouting filthy words at her, the way owners of better cars usually did. She glanced over; the guy was preoccupied with trying to keep his unmuffled engine from stalling out. His Chevy must have been thirty years old, at least— circa 1956, she guessed. No style. At least her old hulk had some style.

The light turned green. Alex pulled away and headed for the garage entrance right across from the main terminal. She turned in, but a barrier was down with a SORRY, ALL FULL sign. Yeah, sure they were sorry. Now she could go all around the oval track again, leave the fucker in some other parking area a mile or more away and how was she supposed to get the suitcase—fuck it. Just fuck it all.

The cold blast of air-conditioning hit her as she struggled into the terminal. Her hair was damp and clinging and inside the pretty silk blouse beat a heart about to explode. She didn't slow down or stop until she got to the ticket lines, which were all, without exception, very long. She wondered how she had gotten singled out for this ever-increasing pileup of shit. She looked for a clock: 3:10.

Dragging the suitcase, she picked a line and joined up. It didn't seem to be moving; other lines, of course, were. She counted the number of people ahead of her. Were couples traveling together to be counted as one or two? She decided to count only the actual number of tickets to be sold before she got there, never mind the accompanying adults, children or pets. Six. Six ahead of her. That wasn't so bad; it only looked like more. She sat down on her suitcase.

A long, long time later, it was her turn. She stepped up to the counter. The reservations clerk flashed a smile, mechanical but hearty, as if she woke up every morning thinking this was the day she'd be discovered. L.A. was full of pretty, vivacious young women expecting to be discovered; Alex liked them, usually, felt sad for them, too. This one had a name badge reading "Cindi." Give it all you've got, Cindi, you never know when a producer or major director might step up to your counter, start to ask for a ticket to San Francisco and stop in his tracks, say, "You've got just the wonderful smile I need to star in my next film," and whip out a contract there and then. In the meantime, Cindi was waiting for Alex to state her business.

"When's your next flight to San Francisco?" Alex asked her.

"On the half-hour. But it's booked."

"I'll take the one after that, then," Alex said. She put her purse up on the counter and started to reach for a credit card.

The clerk shook her shaggy-dog haircut. "That one's booked too," she said, sounding genuinely sorry.

"What about—"

"We're booked solid all day. It's a real mess," Cindi confided in Alex, as if expecting sympathy for her terrible predicament.

Holding down the panic as best she could, Alex utilized all her acting training to keep from screaming. "How about—what d'you call it? stand-in?"

"Standby. You can try. Gate 2-B. But they're like animals today, honestly." Cindi sighed.

A sob escaped from Alex's tightly compressed lips. "Oh, my God," she moaned softly.

"What? What is it?" The clerk was concerned. Nobody in her limited experience had ever looked so close to fainting or bursting out in a fit of crying right on her desk.

Alex could barely talk, but her eyes sought Cindi's, needing a friend. She cast her glance down again and confided in a low, desperate whisper, "I came down to L.A. to see my father . . . he's in a rest home and I'm the only one he recognizes . . . I knew I shouldn't have come, but it was Thanksgiving—" Her voice caught. She raised her eyes again, checking her audience. The clerk was all sad eyes and clucking tongue. Behind her, in the line, there were some rumblings of irritation and impatience.

"Now my husband calls . . ." she went on hesitating just ever so delicately, almost embarrassed to burden a stranger, even such a sympathetic one, with her woe. But she forced herself. "I've been fighting traffic for two hours . . . to tell me she's dying. Her condition was stable when I left San Francisco but now, just suddenly, with no—"

Finally, a little slow on the draw, the shaggy blond girl picked it up. "Who? Whose condition?"

"My daughter. She has cancer of the uterus . . . seventeen years old!"

"Oh, my God."

"Isn't there . . . some way to get me on a flight?" Alex pleaded.

"Oh, honey, let me get my supervisor," the young woman said, almost crying herself. "You take a seat over there." As she stepped away from her position, the line behind Alex bristled angrily. Alex dragged her suitcase to a bench nearby. She sat, suddenly dizzy. All those pills on an empty stomach. She leaned forward with her head in her hands.

"Madam?"

She heard a man's voice from a mile away. Then, abruptly, he was much too close. Murmuring in her ear. "Madam?" Speaking quietly, trained to be tactful. Alex jerked her head up. The man was in a uniform, blue with gold-embroidered epaulettes and brass buttons. He was half-kneeling beside her; no wonder his voice sounded so . . . intimate. Solicitous and patronizing, he leaned closer. What the hell did he want . . .

"I've been told of your situation," he murmured delicately. She couldn't stand his look of pity, and the superiority that always goes with pity—as if he was glad that whatever she had wasn't catching. Her head was reeling. Couldn't he see, didn't anybody care that she had to get out of here, and NOW . . . ?

". . . we'll do everything possible, of course, but there's no procedure whereby we can arbitrarily displace passengers already holding tickets on our San Francisco flight 119 in order to accommodate—"

It got through the vertigo; he was trying to help her, get her on a plane. She cut through the crap. "How about Vegas?" she suggested.

"What?" He seemed bewildered. Slow.

"D'you fly to Vegas?" she snapped impatiently.

The supervisor's eyes hardened. He straightened up, gave her the steeliest look his bland blue eyes could manage, and then turned and walked away.

Alex shouted after him, good and loud, goddamn him. *"Well, do you?"*

After a while the reeling sensation slowed down, or she got used to it, enough to stand up and start dragging the suitcase across the terminal floor again. She got to the door, out into a blast of hellish heat. She found the trusty old Mercedes exactly where she'd left it—double-parked in front of the terminal, trunk lid up. She had blocked a couple of cars at the inside curb, and it looked like the owners were not being good sports about it. Two men were standing by her car, sweating and mad as hell. One was wearing a goddamned pinstriped suit and tie—no wonder he was so hot. The other guy, outfitted in greasy jeans and sleeveless T-shirt, was leaning into her car window and honking the horn over and over and over again. Rude.

She dragged the suitcase over to the trunk. "Oh, God, I'm sorry, you guys," she told them. She waited a hairline second on the chance one of them might want to help her lift it, but no way. They both just stood there sweating and glaring at her furiously. She hoisted the case up and dropped it into the trunk. "Been trying to call the Auto Club," she said. "It just went dead on me." She walked around to get into the car. The fellow who'd been honking her horn stepped back to let her in. Neither seemed to have much to say.

"Let me try it again," she said sweetly. "I think it's the electrical system." The men stood there, mesmerized by their own fury. Maybe her almost jaunty optimism had something to do with it. She was in control again. She smiled brightly at them as she turned the key. The engine rattled to life.

"Well, what d'you know?" she exclaimed. "Must've just needed a rest."

The Mercedes chugged away just as a tow truck pulled in.

The airport traffic crept like alluvial mud, with every crossing light red. It was maddening, and she felt caught—not that she could have said where she wanted to be instead. Out, just out. Out of the goddamned airport, out of the heat, somewhere she could sit quietly and get herself straight and think what to do next. She wanted to put her head down and sleep. The light turned green and she hit the accelerator, just as a taxi was pulling out from a loading zone on her right. She slammed the brakes hard, screeched to a stop. There was an instant echo—another set of brakes behind her, then a sickening crunch of metal.

Alex was thrown forward. Her head slammed against the windshield as the Mercedes, bucked from behind, rammed into the back of the cab. Dazed, she pulled herself up and turned to look behind her. A dark and very angry-looking man was getting out of a dark-green, custom-built Cadillac. Alex turned again and looked forward. The cab driver was coming toward her from the other direction; he looked mad, too.

The owner of the Cadillac leered in at her window. His rage was quiet and intense. "You have no brake lights," he said. If you could bottle that quiet fury you wouldn't need nukes.

Alex tried a kind of sweet, girlish smile. She held up one finger: one brake light was still working. The man didn't think it was funny. Now the cab driver's head appeared right behind him. "You insured?" the cabbie growled unpleasantly. He needed a shave, badly.

Alex steadied her head against the steering wheel. Wasn't *she* the injured party, the lady in the middle, the innocent victim? Shouldn't she have something to accuse somebody else of for a change? After all, it was her nightmare they were butting into.

"Stay with her while I get the police," the man from the custom Caddy told the cabby. He walked away purposefully. The back of his suit jacket was drenched with sweat.

Oh, God, police. ONCE-FAMOUS ACTRESS HANGED

FOR MURDER. Did they still hang people in this state? Had they ever? How did Susan Hayward die in that picture . . . ?

She raised her head and looked straight into the cab driver's watery eyes. "You pulled out right in front of me," she told him, surprising herself with how calm her voice was.

He leaned closer to take a good look at her. His breath smelled of onions. "Don't I know you from somewhere?" he asked. "You look familiar . . ."

A garish symphony of auto horns had started to build behind them. Alex put her head down on the wheel again, as if the headache had just come with the collision. Slowly, unseen, her left hand reached for the door handle, made contact, closed around it. She pulled it back carefully. Abruptly, she threw her weight against the door. It flew open, knocking the cabby to the ground.

Alex grabbed her purse, leaped out and ran. There was a parking structure ahead, and she headed for it. She was surprised that she could still run. She didn't know what she'd do when she got to the car shed, and she wasn't looking back. The cabby was gaining on her. Suddenly he was on her heel; she heard his panting just before he grabbed her arm, hurting her, spinning her around. She slammed her purse against his head, hard, and brought her knee up swiftly. What every young girl should know, and does—not nice, but effective. He groaned loudly and doubled up; she turned and ran again.

Just at the entrance to the parking structure, she turned to look back. He was nearly up to her, hobbling, looking a bit like Quasimodo, backlit. She ran through the parking shed and out into the sunlight on the other side. Gasping for breath, dizzy again and hot, she stopped and looked around, hoping her stomach wouldn't take a clue from her heaving chest.

This was the apse-end of the airport and not much was going on; it was too far from a terminal to get lost in a crowd. Nothing but cars, parked cars, moving cars, cars waiting at red lights, cars starting to crawl at green lights, cars snaking in and out of parking garages, lots, up and down ramps. And one beat-up old Chevy, its primer coat of many colors vaguely familiar, was pulled over on the shoulder of the roadway with its hood up. A man was leaning into it. She ran in a semi-crouch, ducked around behind the Chevy and pulled at the passenger door, which gave her a hard time. It finally gave way and she climbed inside. She looked through the windshield to see the man standing at the open hood with a couple of tools in his hand, staring at her, squinting in the sun. He just watched while she concentrated on catching her breath and trying to look like she'd been sitting there for hours.

He was in his 30's, wearing chinos, an ugly plaid short-sleeved shirt, and run-down cowboy boots. Not bad looking, if a bit on the seedy side. He was muscular with dirty blond hair, amiable-looking, not your brainy type. He came over to the driver's window, leaned on one elbow, looked her over pretty damned thoroughly. As John Wayne might have, he said only, "This may take a little while."

Relieved that he wasn't going to make a big deal

out of it one way or another, she nodded. "That's okay."

He went back under the hood. Alex turned in her seat and glanced through the dirty back window. The cabby was stalking in this direction, and cussing to himself. She scrunched down in the seat, as low as she could. She took off her sunglasses, whipped a scarf from her handbag and tied it around her head. The cabby went right on by, muttering threats to the shimmering air.

The man hollered something at her from under the hood. She couldn't make it out.

"What?" she called out the window.

"Try the starter!"

She reached over to where the starter ought to be but there was only a hole in the dashboard.

"Where is it?" she asked.

He sounded disgusted at her ignorance. "Hangin' below the dash. Look for two wires."

The Chevy was dusty and grimy and smelled less than wonderful under the dashboard. She looked around, found the loose ignition, took it in her left hand, and turned the key with her right. The starter ground reluctantly.

"Gas it! Give 'er some gas!"

Alex scrambled under the wheel, reached for the accelerator with her right foot and gunned it. There was an unbelievable roar and a dense cloud of smoke blew out of the exhaust pipe.

He seemed quite pleased. He dropped the hood with a clank, looked over at her and nodded. She hesitated, nodded back. Thumbs up. She slid back over to the passenger seat. He opened the door, got behind the wheel and slammed the door. It banged and fell back open. He reached out and slammed it again. This time it caught.

He just sat there for a minute, not doing anything, and then, without looking at her, he asked casually, "This a pickup?"

What an ego. She didn't need him and his insults. She grabbed at the door handle on her side, but it was stuck. She was furious. The goddamned door wouldn't open.

"Okay, okay. I was just checking," the guy said mildly. He put the car in gear and rolled toward the exit. Alex settled back in the seat, still on guard.

They got into the barely creeping traffic going around the inner oval of the airport drive. He was facing the wrong way for getting out and would have to snake all the way around before they could finally get clear of the place. "Y'going into L.A.?" he asked.

She didn't answer.

"My name's Turner Smith," he said.

She nodded. "I'm . . . Viveca." She waited but there was no reaction.

"You watch much TV?" she asked him.

He seemed vaguely surprised at the question. "Not much," he said.

They were approaching the scene of her accident. Her Mercedes seemed to be the cause of much of this horrendous traffic jamup; it sat skewered in the center lane between the cab and the Cadillac. There was a crowd standing around and she recognized some of the cast. She ducked below the dashboard as they moved with infinite slowness past the scene.

"My heel's loose," she said by way of explanation. She stayed low, fooling with her shoe.

Turner Smith reported on the scene as they passed. "Spade in a Caddy ran into somebody," he told her.

Alex looked up to see if he was for real, cracking her head on the dash in the process. "Spade-in-a-Caddy?" she repeated scornfully. "Is that anything like Jack-in-the-Box?"

Sarcasm went right over his head. "I'd sure love to have the Caddy dealership in Watts," he said. "Spades spend disproportionately on transportation . . . also on dressing their young."

She couldn't believe this guy. "What're you? The Klan anthropologist?"

He didn't mind the idea. "You can tell a lot about people from the cars they drive," he said.

They were past the accident now, joining the long line of cars on the road out of the airport. Alex sat up. She looked around at the wreck this bigot was driving, with its dashboard wiring hanging down like spaghetti. She could have been strangled or electrocuted under there. He was a fine one to lecture on how you could tell about people from the cars they drive.

"You sure can," she agreed pointedly.

"This? This is an investment," he said.

"Investment?"

"Fix it up a little bit . . . your beaners'll fight with machetes for a car like this."

"My beaners?" She couldn't believe this guy.

He nodded. He did have a pleasant face but what a peabrain . . . "It's the tailfins," he was saying. "Anything late 50's, GM or Chrysler." He glanced

48

at her quickly, not totally insensitive. "You don't say beaners?"

"No."

"On your best behavior, uh?"

There followed a long, unpleasant silence while the Chevy chugged its way through the traffic.

Chapter
Five

HIS INVESTMENT PLODDED THROUGH THE TRAFFIC ON several of its eight cylinders, belching clouds of smoke. Turner leaned across Alex to reach inside the doorless glove compartment. He snapped on an elderly mono tape player and something resembling music blared out cheerfully.

Everything whizzed past them as they klutzed along the slow lane. At the interchange with the Santa Monica Freeway they turned off, heading God knew where. Turner Smith seemed to know, and Alex didn't much care. A drink would clear her head; in the meantime it was all going by without her having to think about anything at all.

The sun had finally started to pull in its horns and dusk was mingling with the smog by the time the Chevy pulled off on an exit in the middle of nowhere.

"Third and Garland," Turner Smith announced.

Alex just turned her head and stared at him. "That's where I'm going," he explained.

"Oh." It started creeping back on her, the load of shit. The trouble she was in. "Okay," she said slowly.

"But I'd be glad to take you—"

"Just drop me where I can get a cab," she said, making a big effort to pull it together. She was going to have to call Jacky again, try to talk him into another course of action. No way was she going to take his first suggestion. Maybe by now he had thought about it and realized calling the cops would be a bad idea. Maybe he would come up with a better thought this time. She'd call him from a bar.

"Whatever makes you happy," Turner Smith said. He was okay, a nice enough guy. She'd lucked out, but now it was time to get rid of him. She wouldn't miss the Chevy, either.

"A cab," she told him. "A cab would make me happy."

He was silent for a minute, concentrating on keeping the motor gasping, and then he said, "Look, it wouldn't be out of my way to take you where you're going."

"How do you know? How do you know where I'm going?" she asked.

They were stopped at a traffic light. He eased the hand-choke out a bit, then in. "Well . . . no place'd be that far out of my way," he said. A genial fellow. He did have a nice smile, a bit crooked, which made it look honest.

He turned back to the road and she studied his profile. It was a nice, rugged, handsome face—kind of boyish, but used. The kind of face that should have lots of friends. How come it was hanging out with nothing to do? And on a national holiday. "Find yourself with a lot of time on your hands, Turner?" she asked, not unkindly.

The light turned green and the Chevy bucked ahead. "Just the Klan meeting this week, that's all I got," Turner said solemnly.

But she had touched on something true in his life. He stole a sideways look at her. She felt him looking, but one of the pills had just let her down and she felt like she was just coming back from a long trip, waking from some kind of trance. She gazed past his head and out the window as if she'd never seen plastic houses and scrawny palm trees before. "What time is it?" she asked with sudden urgency.

"Six thirty".

Nine hours gone! Where? She couldn't believe it. Nine hours since she'd woken up with that . . . man. What had been happening? The whole world could have come crashing down; they might be looking for her. *What had she been doing for this whole goddamned day?* Not helping herself, that was for sure. Running in a tight circle, fucking herself over. Lost her car, her suitcase—anybody could tell she was trying to make a run for it. She looked *guilty*. By now she might be the only person in the whole world who still didn't have a clue about what she'd been doing the night before.

She dug in her purse, found a loose pill. As she popped it and swallowed dry, she had a moment's twinge for the bottles in her lost suitcase.

"Don't you need water?" Turner asked.

She shook her head, no. Her mind was racing

through a swamp of horrors, one possibility more grim than the next. She couldn't think straight at all.

"You're experienced, huh?" Turner was commenting.

"Some things," she agreed. Got to think, got to sort things out. I used to think very, very well. It can't all be gone, not yet. Think. Got to think about that loft—could anybody trace me there? I might have left something. Fingerprints! What did I touch there? Oh, Jesus, what didn't I?

Okay, turn it over slowly and figure it out. It's a holiday. Maybe nobody's missed him, and if they haven't gone looking for him, maybe nobody's found him yet. Maybe it's not too late to pull something off. Pick up after myself, as my mother used to advise . . .

"Third and Garland," she said to Turner. "That's downtown L.A., right?"

"Yeah."

"I've got . . . a friend lives not too far from there," she said. "Maybe you could drop me."

"Whatever makes you happy," he repeated. She looked at him. Funny choice for a favorite expression.

"What were you doing at the airport?" she asked him, idly curious now that he was starting to come into focus.

"Me? Oh, seeing my daughter off. She spent a couple of days with me. I had to get her on a two thirty flight so she'd be back with her mother by turkey time."

"*Two* thirty?" Alex echoed.

"Hung around, I guess," he said, in answer to her unasked question.

53

"I *guess*."

"Used to like to watch takeoffs and landings . . . now, modern airports, you can't see the planes. It's like the bus depot."

Alex smiled. "I haven't heard that in years," she said.

"What?"

"Bus *de*pot."

"That the way they say it where you come from?" he asked with a sidelong glance.

"Yup." She smiled faintly. "Small town in Illinois. Bus *de*pot. So you're a small town boy, too."

"Yup."

He had a nice laugh, restrained, though, as if he couldn't really let go, or hadn't in so long he'd forgotten how. She actually laughed, too. She studied him as he drove. "Well, the airport's as good a place as any for takeoffs and landings, all right," she said. "And on a holiday . . . maybe you liked watching all those people saying goodbye," she suggested gently.

"Maybe." He brightened. "They say hello, too, y'know."

Alex waited but the conversational ball had dribbled to a halt. She turned away and looked out at the unpromising seediness of a row of depression-built tenements. "Gets dark early . . . not even winter yet," she said sadly.

Turner didn't answer. He didn't even ask what she was doing at the airport, for which she was grateful.

They passed a garage and a vacant lot that she thought she recognized. Close enough.

"This'll be fine, right here," she told him.

"Here? You sure?"

It was a deserted street. Just a few flickering blue and red neon window signs: for a reader and advisor, an art gallery, a bar. A neighborhood in transition.

"My friend's right around the corner," Alex assured him.

Turner stopped the car. "What if he's not home?" he asked. He sounded worried about her, that was sweet. But she wished he'd go away now.

"He's home," she promised. "He's sick. Listen, thanks again for the lift." She worked the door handle, but it wouldn't open.

Turner smiled nicely. "Hold the handle back and shove at the same time," he said. "Sometimes it won't stay shut, sometimes it won't open. You got to know how to work it."

Alex tossed her purse down, grabbed the handle with both hands, and pushed. The door flew open. She damn near fell into the street. Pulling up her shredded dignity, she pushed her hair back, straightened her skirt and got out of the car. She reached back inside for her purse, and slammed the door. She stood there and looked at him for a minute. Nice guy, but . . .

"Give one to the Grand Dragon for me," she said.

"You got me all wrong, lady," Turner protested.

"Really?"

He grinned. "Well . . . that's okay. I probably got you wrong, too."

She thought of a couple of things to say, but after a beat she turned and walked toward the bar. She didn't hear the Chevy bump and grind its gears for a takeoff until she was around the corner and out of sight.

* * *

The bar was strictly male, and she got some X-ray eye treatment, but nobody hassled her and she left quickly after bolting down a soda and two vodkas. The streets were dark now, with an oasis of light every now and then—neon, mostly. The art gallery was closed for the holiday; the restaurant offered TURKEY DINNER $5.95. She walked by instinct, until she saw a huge multicolored "Drakula" head lit by three white unshaded garage lights. She turned the next corner onto Mateo Street.

The loft building was a couple of blocks down. There were people on the street now, hanging out, playing radios, talking, a card game in progress inside the open door of a social club. Now and then a couple of kids on skates or banging a rubber ball against a wall. She reached 544 and looked up. Some of the windows were lit, but not the second floor. Alex shivered, hesitated, and stepped up the cracked wide step onto the entranceway. The door was broken and opened easily. The hallway was lit dimly by a single overhead bulb. The stairs loomed just ahead of her. She heard the sounds of a distant television show, canned laughter and then music. As she mounted the stairs, she heard someone practicing the clarinet, in a key that clashed with the TV.

At the door of the second-floor front apartment, she stood listening for sounds from inside. Nothing, she was—almost—sure. She turned the handle and pushed the door open slowly. Not a sound. She went inside.

Nothing had changed, although in the semi-darkness, with moonlight streaming through the windows, and new shadows everywhere, the loft had a very different aspect. She didn't look toward the bed. The blue-eyed cat came trotting out of the kitchen to wrap himself around her legs, meowing loudly. She bent down to pet him: warm and alive. She could feel his heart beating under the soft fur.

She shut and bolted the door. She closed the blinds, darkening the room to an even more sinister depth of shadow with each window. She moved quickly, and when the windows were secured she switched on a lamp.

The silence was quadrophonic.

She went into the kitchen, switched on the over-head light, and found the utility closet. Doubling her pace now, she pulled out a pail, brush, mop, a couple of bottles and shakers of cleaning stuff, and a pair of rubber gloves. The loft was large and the job was formidable. How do you clean away traces of yourself when you don't know where you've been . . . ?

She stopped only twice in her preparations, once to pour herself a drink and once to open a can of catfood.

Suddenly, standing in the middle of the kitchen, she could have sworn she felt someone watching her. With the outsized, bright yellow gloves on her hands, holding the mop and pail, she stood paralyzed for a moment. She looked through the kitchen doorway toward the bed. The corpse lay sprawled on the white and rust-colored sheets.

"Stay there, okay?" she whispered. "I don't need any help." After a minute, still unable to move, she said, "If I did that to you, I didn't mean it. I swear to God I'm not a bad person."

He didn't answer, not that she wanted him to. But

breaking the silence between them reduced her tension. "I'll just . . . tidy up," she said, in a reasonable, housewifely tone of voice. "You go on with . . . whatever you were doing."

She moved slowly toward the bed. Gingerly, she pulled the bloody sheet off, wadded it up and dropped it in the middle of the room. And then she went on automatic. She was a very good cleaner, trained in early girlhood by a mother who was a fanatic. Strip the bed, pillowcases, towels—any laundry she might have touched went onto the pile in the middle of the floor. Every surface got scrubbed with ammonia and a hard brush until it shone—tiles, linoleum, formica, bathroom, kitchen . . . and every time she took a drink the glass went into the dishwasher. She sponged the faucets and then threw the sponge in the dishwasher, too. Down on her knees with a folded towel for a cushion, her hair wrapped in the scarf she'd had around her neck, Alex worked like the white tornado until the place was damned near sparkling.

She'd take the garbage with her, dump it (cat food can, Scotch bottle once it was empty) someplace safe. After a while, the alcohol warmed her blood so that she felt calm and in control. Now she could look at Bobby Marshack's body with less shock and more sympathy. "Look," she said at one point, pausing as she worked near him, "if I did do it, you must've got me crazy. Called me a lush, did you? Something crazy like that?"

She stared at him but he didn't answer. Abruptly she went back to business, pulling off the pillow on which she had slept, replacing it with a fresh one she'd found in the linen closet. She wiped the windowsill with a damp towel, then wiped off the lampshade and every item on the dresser. She stepped back, looked around: had she missed anything?

Apparently not. The dead man lay on a bare mattress and every other thing she could think of had been cleaned. She was about to turn off the lamp—still with the yellow rubber gloves on—when suddenly she remembered something. She went over to his jacket, took the wallet out of his pocket, wiped it off, took out the credit cards and—just to be on the safe side—bills, wiped each item carefully and replaced it. Then she turned off the lamp and pulled open the blinds.

"I'll get the windows next time," she said, joking to herself. She glanced around the room one final time, all clear, all clean—and then something hit her with a bolt—moonlight was glinting off the steel blade in Bobby Marshack's chest.

She moved back toward the bed in a cold sweat of renewed horror. She stood staring down at it. She had to do it.

She pulled the scarf from her head, carefully wound it around the handle of the knife—which wobbled at her touch. She pulled it out, gagging as the steel cut through the gray, yielding flesh. She had to wait to find out if she was going to be sick . . . after a minute, she thrust the knife and the rubber gloves and her scarf into the pillowcase. She took the pillowcase to the center of the room where the pile of laundry was heaped. She started to stuff the dirty sheet and towels into the pillowcase, but suddenly she sensed something behind her, another presence in the room. She stiffened, bent over the laundry, and listened.

Nothing. Her imagination. She straightened up, turned around slowly. Nothing. She finished stuffing the pillowcase, checked the bathroom one last time and flipped off the light with the side of her arm that was covered by her jacket sleeve. On her way back, she stopped at the phone, unclipped it from the cord, took it into the kitchen and dropped it in the dishwasher. She poured in some detergent and started the machine on HOT WASH CYCLE.

She picked up the stuffed pillowcase and headed for the door. The cat meowed—but where the hell was it? "Kitty?" she called. A louder meow—coming from the closet. Alex went over to the closet door, put her hand on the knob and started to turn it. The cat meowed again.

The cat was *behind a closed door.*

Chapter
Six

HOW DID THE CAT GET IN THE CLOSET? AND *WHO* shut the door after him?

Her eyes fixed on the closet, Alex managed somehow to pull her scarf from the bag of laundry, wrap it around her left hand, and grab the knob of the front door. She opened it with excruciating slowness, expecting the closet door to fly open at any moment. She moved out into the hallway, and pulled the apartment door shut with her wrapped hand. She exhaled deeply, unaware until now that she'd been holding her breath. As she turned around, she bumped into the shadowy hulk of a man.

Her scream was muffled, with no strength behind it. The man clutched at her arms. Her legs turned to jello. But the man had a pleasant face, and he was holding her tenderly. Turner Smith.

He looked concerned. She thought he might apologize for giving her the fright of her life, but no. What he said was, "How is he?"

". . . Who?" Alex's heart was pounding, hard. She let herself lean against Turner Smith for just a minute, to catch her breath.

"Your sick friend."

Oh, yeah. "He's better," she said. She tested her breathing, and then moved away from him, onto her own two feet. She wanted to get the hell away from that door, that loft, that neighborhood. The city, if possible, and then the country, the world. But definitely this building, first. She brushed past Turner, heading for the stairs. He followed right behind her, talking all the way.

"You're a lady with a lot on her mind," he observed. Brilliant.

She kept on going. They were in the front hallway before she answered. "What d'you mean?"

"Well . . . I mean, don't you kind of wonder how I found you?"

Must have been something else on her mind. No, she hadn't wondered. She pulled open the door to the street and held it for him. Now she was wondering. He handed her a wallet—hers.

"Must've dropped out of your purse. Had your friend's address on that matchbook." Alex pushed the door open and stepped outside. She held out her hand and he gave her the wallet. She didn't look at it, just took it in the same hand that still had her scarf wrapped around it. She looked at him. In the cracked light of a streetlamp that had been used for target practice, she could just make out his profile. All-American boy, once; now scarred and hard. She studied him, vaguely suspicious. Was he playing some kind of weird game with her?

"You do his laundry for him?" Turner was asking, looking down pointedly at the stuffed pillowcase she was carrying.

Alex nodded. "All the time."

"You don't look that domesticated to me," he observed.

"I'm not," she told him. "I'm . . . just a good friend."

She started to walk toward the Chevy, parked right at the curb. It was the only transport in sight. He ambled alongside. "Must be nice, having a good friend," he said.

She turned and looked at him, full-face in the moonlight now. "You lonely, sailor?" she asked wryly.

He leaned down, grabbed the passenger door handle with both hands. One pushed, one pulled and the door came open. He stepped back to let her in. "No," he told her. "But I sure don't have anybody doin' my laundry, either."

She tossed the pillowcase onto the back seat and climbed in. "Poor thing," she said. He went around to the driver's seat. "Where's this small town you come from?" she asked him. She didn't give a damn, really, but chatting kept her mind off the cat in the closet and the other conundrums of her life. For the moment.

"Bakersfield." Turner held the wires and turned the starter and pumped the gas and the Chevy whined and sighed and started.

"No wonder," Alex said.

"And you're L.A. by way of the Big Apple," he guessed.

They were getting away, off this street and heading for the tall buildings that twinkled against the dark. He was wrong, but she let it go.

She had never made it to New York. That was where the stage was, the only stage that counted. For years she told herself that she wasn't afraid, that it just hadn't come up: she was too busy making films (not movies) here and in Europe. She didn't lie so much to herself any more; of course she was afraid. Broadway was for people with real guts. She no longer even said "maybe someday . . ." L.A. was her home, and her punishment. Suddenly she wanted a drink very, very desperately.

"Where we heading, Turner?"

"Where do you want to go?"

"Home."

"Okay."

He drove for a while and then he said, "Y'know, you hurt me a little bit, that thing before. About the Klan."

Alex shrugged. "You're really with the American Civil Liberties Union?"

He shook his head. "I'm not a joiner," he said seriously.

"No shit."

"You got a mouth," he told her, more as an observation than a judgment.

Suddenly, deliberately abrupt, out of nowhere, he asked her sharply, "What kind of friend, you need to have his address on a matchbook? Wouldn't you know it by heart?"

Off-balance, Alex answered defensively. "Maybe he just moved."

Turner thought about it and nodded, apparently accepting this. But then he asked her, "Did he?"

"Or maybe I've got amnesia." Alex was getting annoyed. What the hell was this? How come her business was his business all of a sudden? Maybe there was no such thing as a free ride, but she didn't have to answer to him, this guy wearing a really awful short-sleeved plaid shirt. His arms were tan and firmly muscled, with sandy hairs catching the lights of the Freeway.

He wasn't ruffled by her tone. *"Have* you got amnesia?" he asked.

She looked away from his glance. "Sometimes," she told him truthfully.

He didn't say anything more until they got to the Beverly Hills exit and turned off. "You above Sunset or below?"

Her voice came out husky. "Below."

She directed him to her street and they clattered into the driveway. The Chevy groaned like an old mule as Turner switched off the ignition.

"Thanks," Alex said. "Again."

"Any time," Turner said.

She let go her purse to push-pull the door open, stepped down and started to reach for the laundry. But Turner grabbed it first. "I'll take it," Alex told him firmly, reaching for it.

He was already getting out of the car, hauling the bag in one hand. "That's okay. I'll carry it to the door for you."

She didn't want him to pick up on how apprehensive she felt. She was jumpier than she had ever been in her life, and with damned good reason. She needed to be alone, inside where she could have a long slow cool drink and call Jacky. But Turner Smith didn't seem to know when to exit. He was right behind her as she turned the key of the front door to her apartment building and started down the carpeted hall.

"What do you do for work, Turner?" she asked him, newly curious.

"I'm a cop."

He didn't see the rush of panic on her face. She was ahead of him, almost at the door of her ground floor apartment. He went right on explaining. "Ex-cop, really. Disabled."

He's not after me, was her first thought. They wouldn't send a guy like that in a Chevy like that all by himself after a dangerous killer like me. He's an ex-cop, anyway. *Ex*-cop.

"You don't look disabled to me," she said. They had reached her apartment door, and she turned around to face him. It was true; he looked strong and healthy. Young and handsome and strong and healthy.

"I'll take that as a compliment," he said, smiling a little.

She nodded and reached out her hand for the laundry. "Well, good night." She took it from him. "I'd invite you in but . . . it's too ethnic, the neighborhood."

He nodded. "I know. Jewish. Very stable real-estate, low turnover."

"Exactly."

"Helps them keep certain traditional values . . ."

66

"Turner . . ."

He charged right on. ". . . real heavy emphasis on education achievement and in the arts . . ."

"Please," she begged. She wanted to stop the jokes and just get inside where she could cool down.

"But that kind of isolation does breed prejudice, and—"

"*Turner.*"

He relented. He was smiling at her, just a hint of an honest, friendly smile. But Alex wasn't having any. God, she was tired! It had been some day, after all . . .

"I've got a little disappearing act, where I count to three . . . and *you* disappear," she said quietly.

"Oh."

He waited, like someone on the receiving end of a knife-throwing act.

"One . . ." Alex counted. "Thanks for helping me today."

"You're welcome," he said.

"Two . . . you really did save my life."

He nodded. "Any time," he said.

"Three . . . goodbye," Alex said, not unkindly.

"Sure," Turner agreed, but he just stood there nicely, not moving.

Alex turned the key in the lock, opened her door and let herself in. She closed the door behind her and dropped the heavy pillow case on the floor. She leaned against the first available wall and breathed deeply. She looked around the dark living room, and down at the bulging pillowcase. She turned and yanked the door open. There was Turner, standing exactly where she had left him.

"Didn't work," he said.

Alex smiled wanly, not sure whether she was glad or sorry. "Sometimes it doesn't, when I'm tired." They looked at each other for a second. Then she said, "What the hell, come on in, there's a couple of tacos in the freezer."

She snapped on the lights and led the way inside.

He looked around as they moved across the living room and into the kitchen. He went to the fridge and opened the freezer compartment. "That's what you got, all right," he reported. "Two tacos."

"Have I ever lied to you?" Alex answered wearily.

"Very weird," Turner commented from deep inside the fridge.

She bristled. "What's weird?"

"Two tacos, a jar of olives, and six and a half jars of mayonnaise."

"I always think I'm running out," she explained.

He continued the inventory. "And possibly . . . I think it was a lettuce once. Or a lime."

"I don't cook," Alex said.

With no pause he went on with the list: ". . . and four gallons of Thunderbird."

"It was on special."

He straightened up and closed the forlorn refrigerator. He looked at her. "All your credit cards have expired . . ." At her reaction he explained, "I noticed, in your wallet. But . . . there are millionaires out there who wish they had as much mayonnaise as you've got. Any plans for tonight?"

He was really something. "Yeah," she told him. "I'm going to take a shower. The air conditioner in this apartment has been broken for a month."

Turner nodded. "Okay, take the shower. I'll be right back."

"What for?" she asked, puzzled.

"You look like you need some real food," he said. He held out his hand to her. "Give me the key, to get back in."

Alex hesitated. She didn't need a bossy jerk of a cowboy ex-cop from Bakersfield in her life just now. She especially didn't need him taking care of her, trying to make her eat when she didn't want to . . . and suddenly she realized that she was ravenously hungry. And for some dumb, probably self-destructive, reason, she trusted him. What the hell, could she get in any more trouble than she was in already? She picked up the key from the table where she'd tossed it. He took it from her and left.

She stared at the door for a second or two. Who the hell *was* this guy?

But she was too tired and too frazzled to think about anything so complex. There were worse things than giving an ex-cop the key to your apartment. She could name a lot of worse things right off the bat if she wanted to bother. Fuck it. She dropped her clothes on the bedroom floor, stepped into the shower and gave the hot water handle a violent twist.

Chapter
Seven

TURNER CAME BACK LOADED WITH TWO GROCERY BAGS. He set them down on the kitchen counter, opened the fridge, and took out the olives and a jar of mayo. When he opened the olives, he took one quick look at the exotic life going on inside the jar, screwed the top back on tightly, and tossed it in the garbage. He opened a loaf of Wonder Bread from one of his bags, and then set out the rest of the food he'd brought. He unwrapped a package of sliced turkey, put the meat on two fresh slices of bread. He scooped cranberry sauce out of two pleated paper cups and arranged it expertly on the two china plates he found in the cupboard. His movements were quick and easy; he was comfortable in kitchens, used to taking care of himself. He found silverware and glasses, and even a tray to put everything on. He carried the loaded tray out into the living room.

He could hear the hair dryer going as he passed

the closed bedroom door. He set the tray down on the coffee table and opened the sliding glass doors. The patio was small and obviously rarely used. It was walled from its neighbors and filled with a strong scent of night flowers. There was no furniture out there, no table, not even a chair. He went back in, sized up the dining table and started to maneuver it outside.

He went back for the extras—a bottle of wine and a couple of white tapered candles he'd bought on impulse. He had figured she'd have candlesticks and of course she did—real silver. He struck a match and lit the candles. The table looked pleasant, appetizing and even—oh, shit, romantic. Was it foolish? He was about to blow out the candles when he heard the bedroom door open. He straightened up as Alex came out. He stepped back and looked at her. A major improvement.

She had taken trouble. Her hair was soft and brushed to a gleaming thickness; skillfully applied mascara outlined her gray-green eyes. She had done some magic to make the lines disappear; she looked young and expectant, like a girl on a date, almost. She was wearing a very good-looking, expensive dressing gown, not fancy but well draped on her sensationally slim body. She looked like a movie star—no visible flaws, and aware of the impression she was making.

Alex looked out to the patio and the dining table that crowded it, took in the candles and open-faced turkey sandwiches and wine. She was touched, he could tell. The relief he felt at her pleasure astonished him. They stood there looking at each other for a minute, suddenly self-conscious.

She walked over to the patio door and stood next to him. There wasn't much room between the dining table and the sliding glass doors. She didn't seem to know what to say. She just stood there and looked at the table, and looked at him, and he just stood there and waited for her to say something, only it didn't look as if she was going to say anything, so he said, "Only turkey they had was processed."

"That's fine . . ." What the hell was the matter with her, she felt like a sixteen-year-old with a crush. It was this corny setting—candlelight under the stars that had even this big ex-cop bigot looking good, acting sweet and sexy . . . she reached for a glass and took a delicate sip of the wine. She looked for something to distract her. ". . . and cranberries!" she exclaimed inanely.

Turner grinned and pulled out a chair for her. "Hell, you got to have cranberries," he said.

They began to eat—to dine—almost elegantly, on their best behavior, except that she couldn't think of anything to say, and apparently neither could he. It was getting painful. She was usually non-stop gregarious, adept at turning the charm on at will . . . but it had been a heavy day, and this preposterous dinner was so unreal . . . still, it was getting hard to swallow in the silence. She tried. "It's very hot, isn't it? For so late in November."

He nodded. "Yeah, it really is."

They finished their turkey. Alex concentrated on the wine, starting to feel better. The silence between them wasn't so bad, really—maybe it was what she'd heard called "companionable silence," the good kind. Anyway, she relaxed. The candles burned down and started to sputter in their melted wax.

Alex held her wineglass up to the light, admiring the pretty crystal, the deep red glow of the wine, the ruddy, earnest face of the ex-cop across the table.

"It's a trifle fruity," she commented, critically holding the glass with the dark red up against the dying candlelight. "Lacks depth, but for the bucks you can't beat it. You married, Turner?"

You could take him by surprise, but apparently, you couldn't ruffle him. "Who'd marry a guy with a '56 Chevy?"

She looked at him, appraising. "It's an investment . . ." she quoted. "How'd you get disabled?"

Turner shrugged. "It was just an . . . incident."

"Well, you really let it all hang out, don't you?" she laughed.

"Okay. I was knifed by a little hooker, fourteen years of age."

Alex nodded. "Little spic hooker, was she?" It was a taunt, a challenge.

He rose to it. "See!!!! I didn't say anything about spic."

"What stopped you?" Alex asked him. If she kept remembering what a narrow-minded prejudiced tight-ass he was, she could minimize the probability of waking up in bed with him. No more of *that*, at least not this week . . .

"Well," Turner was saying, "she happened to be of Scotch-Irish extraction."

"Oh."

"But you're right," Turner went on. "Most of 'em are Chicano. I didn't invite them in."

"You wouldn't," she retorted.

Turner started to say something and then backed

73

off. "Hey, come on," he said with a little half-smile, "it's Thanksgiving."

Alex raised her wineglass. "I'll drink to that," she said, and did.

"Anyway . . . she must've cut some nerves, up here," Turner told her. He pointed to his chest and upper arm, leading down to his gun hand. "I can't draw my weapon any more, feels awkward . . ."

He trailed off, expecting something, maybe sympathy. He probably got it every other time he'd told his story. But Alex just studied him for a long moment. Then she said, quietly, "Maybe you just got tired of being a cop."

"You kidding?" Turner burst out. "It was the best job I ever had."

Alex took a sip of the wine. "Sure. Hassling drunks and hookers, speed-traps . . . must've been a good life."

"I did investigation work, too. I might've made detective. I was good," he said. Not boasting, not crying about it, kind of matter-of-fact. She believed him.

"Was it here in L.A.?" she asked.

He shook his head. "Back in Bakersfield. Seven years."

She didn't like what she was feeling, all of a sudden. "Is that where you studied bigotry?" she asked coldly.

He wasn't going to fight her. His protest was gentle. "Hey, I'm no bigot."

"No, huh?"

"I just . . . I've been around, that's all."

"All the way to Sacramento, I'll bet," she jibed.

"Yeah . . . and it happens to be the capital of California!"

Alex smiled. "I thought Fresno."

He shook his head. "You're bad," he told her. He thought for a minute or two and then he said, with the air of a Supreme Court Justice in a reasonable mood, "How could I be a bigot? I mean, they're all full of ill-will . . . and malice. I just . . . make observations."

That was outrageous. "Like spade, beaner and spic!"

Turner grinned. "Sounds like a law firm, doesn't it? Spade, Beaner and Spic, good morning!"

"You've got some bent view of the world, Turner!" Alex informed him.

"Comin' from who? A broad with a hundred gallons of cheap wine and two frozen tacos in her icebox?"

"Let's not forget the mayonnaise," Alex contributed.

It was an armed truce—but brief. With tipsy dignity, Alex changed the subject. "Actually, I'm surprised I don't look familiar. Obviously, you don't watch the better TV channels."

He was completely at a loss. "Huh? What?"

She leaned across the table to fix him with her famous eyes. "I'm an actress," she said. And then, with compulsive honesty, she added, "was."

He didn't seem impressed, but he was interested. His bright eyes lit up. "I was even good," she went on. "They were grooming me to be the new Vera Miles."

"The new who?" he asked.

"Exactly!" she exclaimed. "I was meant to replace somebody the audience didn't know was missing. I ought to call Jacky." She was allowing herself to be a bit drunker, disconnected.

Turner was trying to follow. "Call who?"

"Jesus, Turner, don't you know *anybody*? What do you *do* all day, now that you can't—" She pantomimed a quick draw.

"Me? I do plenty."

"Name one," Alex demanded.

"I like to repair stuff," he said.

She laughed. "Stuff? What stuff?"

"Whatever needs it. Whatever people are through with."

That was an unfortunate turn of phrase, she thought. Was she one of his discarded fix-me-ups . . . to hell with it. She finished off the wine in her glass and poured another, full up. She raised a toast. "The good ol' days," she said. "They sure went quick." She drank deeply.

"Were you really any good?" he asked.

"I coulda been a contender," she said, aping Brando.

Turner thought hard. "Hey, I think I did see you in a movie once . . ."

"Thanks."

The phone rang. "Who's at?" she sang out drunkenly, turning toward the open glass doors. It rang again. "Hol' the fort," she told it. She finished off her wine and got unsteadily to her feet; bumping into the table made her giggle. She straightened up and reached for the wine bottle, refilled her glass, and took it with her as she steered a jagged course through the patio doors into the living room and over to the desk where the phone sat, patiently ringing on and on.

"Hello!" she sang out. "Yeah, how y'doin', Jacky? . . . What matter? . . . Oh, yeah, *that* . . ." She glanced out at Turner, still seated at the table. "Uh . . . that matter's all been taken care of, thanks for asking . . . What I mean? . . . I fixed it, it's all-l-l-l better . . . huh? . . . Just a sec." She covered the mouthpiece and yelled out to Turner, "I'm gonna take this in the bedroom."

She put the receiver down, picked up her drink and disappeared into the bedroom. A second later she reappeared. She waved graciously at him, a sweeping gesture that ended up including the bar.

"Just help y'self, Turner!"

She went into the bedroom and closed the door. Picking up the phone, she pulled the long cord over to the bed, and lay down with the phone cradled against her head.

"Hi, Jacky, me again . . ."

"For Christ's sake, Alex, you're drunk again!"

Nothing made her madder than accusations of being drunk, especially when it was true. Her rage boiled up and over reflexively, before she had time to think. Being called a lush was the only thing that made her madder. "Who's drunk?!??!" she exploded, and then immediately calmed down. "C'mon baby, aren't we pals? So what'd *you* do for Thanksgiving?" she cooed at him.

"Alex, I really can't believe it. I really can't . . ."

"What, hon? What can't you believe?"

"Was that bullshit about waking up with a stiff?

77

Was that some kind of joke? Did you get Thanksgiving mixed up with April Fool's Day or something? What the hell's going on with you, Alex?"

"Oh, yeah," she murmured apologetically. "Slipped my mind."

"Jesus Christ, I don't believe it. You wake up with a dead guy and you don't remember fuckin' A about it and it *slips your mind?* What're you, brain-damaged finally, the booze has pickled your fucking *brain?*"

"Don't get mad," she protested weakly, wearily.

Jacky was making the big effort to calm himself down, for her sake. He was sweet. Alex yawned and hoped he hadn't heard it over the phone. He was trying to help her. "What are you going to do, Alex?"

"Nothing much," she said, yawning again. "Just got some laundry to do."

"Alex, listen to me. Fuck the laundry, you know what I'm saying? That's not important. Other things are important, not the laundry. You have things you have to do tonight, you've got to save your ass, Alex. You hear me?"

"Yes, I hear you. No laundry tonight. I'll do it tomorrow."

"Get some sleep, okay? Don't go anywhere or talk to anyone, just get some sleep and when you wake up try not to hit the sauce first thing. You gotta have your head on straight for a while now . . . Alex?"

But she was sound asleep, with his soothing, sexy voice still in her ear.

Out on the patio, Turner sat for a while, and then got restless. He stood up, wandered in to the living room. He pulled the glass doors shut, went to turn on the air conditioner. Nothing. He tapped it, toggled a few switches. He pulled off the plastic face-plate and poked inside. He thought he saw what might be wrong, but he didn't have tools. He went over to the desk to find a letter-opener. The telephone receiver was emitting a high-pitched mechanical whine. He put it to his ear and listened for a minute, and then he hung up the phone.

He went over to the bedroom door. Not a sound. He knocked, no answer. He pressed the door open a crack, then wider, and went in. Passed out on the bed, Alex lay with her head on the pillow, hair spread out in a soft aura of light. The phone was nestled under her chin. Gently, he took it from her pillow and replaced the receiver on its stand. Then he sat down on the bed next to her.

He studied her composed, peaceful and quite lovely face. He wanted to touch her soft pale hair, but he didn't. After a moment he got up and went into the bathroom. He looked around, refolded a crumpled wet towel neatly. He closed the shower door. He stared at the mirrored medicine cabinet and decided not to open it. He turned off the light.

After another long look at Alex, he turned off the bedroom lamp, too. He went out into the patio, cleared away the dishes and glasses and moved the table back inside. He cleaned up the kitchen. At the front door, he made sure the patent lock was on, and her key was on the table where she would see it. He let himself out.

A curtain fluttered at the patio door, slightly ajar.

Chapter
Eight

THE WAKE-UP HEADACHE WAS BRUTAL. WINE WAS sometimes worse than hard stuff the next day. Her head felt over-inflated, about to burst; the little demons pounding to get inside her skull were using machetes along with their usual hammers. It was time to go through another entry into the hell of being awake. Not that unconsciousness had been so marvelous—no forgetfulness this time, but an ominous residue of horror from unremembered dreams. She thought briefly, as she always did, of going on the wagon.

One thing at a time. First, figure out where she was . . . The sounds were traffic noises, nothing heavy, your regulation street sounds. The daylight against her lids was hard and painful, but not direct sun, thank God. She was on her back—she stretched out an arm, tentatively—nobody there. Good. Good girl, Alex. She opened her eyes, slowly, one at a time.

She was in her new white dressing gown. The night slowly began to weave into focus. She hoisted herself back, gingerly, against the headboard, half-sitting. Suddenly she leaped up and headed blindly for the bathroom. She got there half-crawling. She stood against the sink, gripping its cool hard smoothness with both fists. She eyed the toilet bowl, but after a time it seemed possible that she was not going to throw up after all.

She raised her head, looked in the mirror. It was awful. Dark roots indicated that she was way overdue—oh, God, how long has it been obvious? Had she really lost her ability to see herself clearly? Welcome to the world of self-delusion, home of the lush and the loopy. She had a hideous flash of herself in a limp, faded blue prison dress, with her dyed hair growing out in patches, being prayed over by a priest and led to the electric chair for something she couldn't remember . . .

Help, she said silently to the mirror. Oh, God, help me. But she had parted company with God too many years before. She was being maudlin, not her style. With a gigantic effort, Alex grinned at her reflection. "Hello-o-o, *Gor*geous." She was Barbra Streisand doing Fanny Brice.

She couldn't sustain it. She was terrified. Tears clouded her vision of herself and she stared down into the cold white sink. "Awwww, God . . ."

She opened the medicine cabinet—nothing but aspirin. She tossed four tablets into her mouth and filled her cupped hands with water to wash them down. She shuddered at the taste. But she thought she might pull through. The day was starting off lousy, but a whole hell of a lot better than the day befo—

Alex opened the shower door. Bobby Marshack lay there, doubled over, staring at her with his dead eyes wide open.

The sound that Alex made was more animal than human. It grew louder as she scrambled backward away from the bathroom. She lost her balance and fell a couple of times as she propelled herself out of there, but she kept retreating, scrambling frantically on her hands and knees. Frantic, she made her mad way like a blind crab, blundering into furniture, walls, knocking over a lamp. She kept making inhuman sounds, groaning and whining and yelping in the grip of horror.

The thought came to her that someone might still be in her apartment. She tried to get to her feet, but could only manage a crouch. Cramped over with fear, she made her way into the kitchen. No one. Back to the living room, no one. The closet near the front door was open, just a crack. That was his favorite place, wasn't it, closets near the front door . . . She backed over to the door, groping with her hand for the knob. She found it, jerked the door open wide. She wasn't even aware that she was still making a deep-throated, growling sound as she ran down the hallway—the white dressing gown flying open, unheeded—and out into the grounds of the building.

The Japanese gardener stopped his work to stare at her. He had been watering and thinning the dichondra until he was distracted by the muffled sound of screams from inside the building. Now he saw this lady flying toward him with her kimono open. He just stood and stared.

Alex saw him, and resisted her first impulse—to throw herself onto him and beg him to take her away, anywhere away from here. Tokyo would be fine—but at his frightened look, she checked herself and backed away from him. She clutched her gown around herself, switched directions and ran toward the street.

A police car was slowly cruising toward her. The cop in the passenger seat was reading the numbers on the houses; she could see his lips move. Alex dashed inside her building. It wasn't the entrance she usually used and she didn't know anyone in this part of the complex. She leaned against the wall and caught her breath. From the hall window she saw the police car pull up in front of the entrance to her wing of the building. Both cops got out and started walking up the path.

"Oh, God . . ." Alex moaned. She ran, in blind panic, down the hallway and out another door. She kept on going across the lawn until she hit the sidewalk. She didn't think the cops saw her. Where were they heading? Who tipped them off? *Who* was following her everywhere with Bobby Marshack's dead body? And why, why, *why?*

She stumbled along the sidewalk, sobbing and gasping for breath. The air was intensely hot and heavy—no aid to breathing in the best of cases. She couldn't make it. Slumping to the grass, she grabbed onto a small stake that supported a little tree at the edge of someone's curb. Alex sank to her knees; it was as far as she could go.

Her own labored breathing and the pounding of her heart kept her from hearing the clunk of Turner's old Chevy at first. Then she did hear it, and looked up and it was actually there, slowing to a stop alongside where she had collapsed. Alex somehow found the energy to get up on her feet again, and start running. Down the sidewalk, blind, furious, weeping uncontrollably, her nose running and her head exploding, she ran.

Turner loped after her. He picked up speed, and managed to grab her hand. Her momentum jerked her around and up against his chest. Alex struggled wildly to get away from him. He tightened his arms around her, pulled her down onto the curb. He held her until, gradually, she gave up the struggle.

They sat for a while right there, his arm tightly around her shoulders. When her sobs subsided, and her trembling was under control, they looked back down the block behind them. More police cars had arrived, blocking off the street. Cops were going into her building. It took a while for Alex to be able to talk. When she could, she said, "I need a drink."

Turner nodded, helped her to her feet. He held her closely and helped her into the Chevy. She was shaky. The cops paid no attention to what was going on down the block from them. Turner made a U-turn and drove noisily off to the nearest liquor store, to which Alex directed him. She sat in the car and waited while he went in. He came out with two six-packs of beer.

"This okay?"

She nodded, not yet ready for extensive conversation. She looked away deliberately as he detached a can from the plastic holder and popped it open. She took it from him casually—too casually—hiding her desperate need. She drank slowly, even daintily, just concentrating on keeping it down.

Only then was she able to ask, "What were you doing there?"

"I was going to fix your air conditioner," he told her.

Her look was full of doubt, suspicion . . . so he nodded toward the back seat. She swiveled slowly around to look—there was a toolbox and a filter for an air-conditioning unit.

"I saw last night that it's only the filter," he said. "You let it get so dirty it was icing up the works." He paused, and then said, less gently, "You're going to tell me what's going on."

He kicked over the engine without waiting for an answer. They pulled out of the parking lot while Alex popped the top of a second can of beer. Her dressing gown was rumpled from being slept in, streaked with dirt and grass stains from sitting on the curb. She was barefoot and had no makeup on, and her dark-rooted hair was tangled and unbrushed. She had left her purse behind and had no choice but to trust this yokel with the Chevy who had a blessed way of turning up just when she most needed him.

She told him, slowly and hesitatingly, but straight, as he drove to MacArthur Park and parked where nobody would disturb them. She got as far as the cat in the closet before he said a word. ". . . and there was somebody in the apartment when I went back," she told him, shivering despite the mounting morning heat.

"You saw somebody?" he asked carefully.

Alex shook her head. "No. But he was there, and

he was watching me. From inside the closet. All the time I was looking for the cat, he was watching me."

"Who? Why do you say *he?"*

"I don't know," she said morosely.

"Whose cat was it?"

"I don't know."

"Whose cat was it?"

"Somebody's cat, a damned blue-eyed cat!"

"Where is it now?" Turner wanted to know.

"How the hell do I know? On *Broadway!"* She waited for his next question, but he didn't say anything. "I got out of there," she said.

He was thoughtful. "You say you saw the dead guy on TV. You sure?"

Alex knew what he meant. Maybe she had seen him someplace else, in a kind of fog of her own, and couldn't really remember straight. Maybe she'd only dreamed she'd seen him on TV when in fact, she had been a lot closer to him than that . . . she wasn't angry, it was a fair question. She answered him straight: "I'm sure. He was taking pictures of ladies with biceps and string bikinis . . . and there was a lot of loud music."

"That's all you know about the guy? He took dirty pictures?"

"Yes."

"That, and the fact that you took him to bed with you," Turner went on, not nicely.

"He took *me!"* Alex protested. "It wasn't my apartment!" Then she wondered, as he probably did, why she was trying to make such a fine distinction. "It happens," she said.

Turner nodded. Then, oddly compassionate, not

nasty at all, he said, "Must just be your way of making friends."

But she was hurting, and not hearing nuances, and anyway it was hard to recognize sincerity when you seldom ran across it. "Is that a crack?" she charged. But looking sideways at him, she realized that he was trying to be nice, in his own way. As she relaxed, the leash on her memory loosened a bit, and random thoughts passed by. Thoughtfully, she snared one. "Funny," she mused out loud, "I didn't like him."

"I guess you didn't," Turner agreed, thinking, no doubt, of the knife.

Alex shook her head. "I mean on TV," Alex said. "He put me off. Unpleasant fellow, I was thinking when I saw him." She was quiet for a moment, thinking hard. Then she said, with slow emphasis, "I wouldn't have gone to bed with him."

Turner tossed her a sideways glance. "You did, though."

She nodded. "I know. But . . . it's funny, all the same."

"Not funny," Turner said. "You black out, don't you?"

She hated it. She wanted to deny it. But . . . how could she? She'd already admitted that she didn't remember that night at all. She just didn't answer him.

There were all kinds of silences. This one was unpleasant. Then Turner said, "Want my advice? Turn yourself in to the cops."

Alex stared straight ahead, through the dusty windshield at the trees. "I can't," she said.

"What d'ya mean?"

"I won't," she amended. "Listen, how about driving me to Santa Monica, and then you can just get out of this whole mess and forget it. Okay?"

"What's in Santa Monica?"

"A friend."

"You've got a lot of friends. Don't need me, huh?"

"It's not that, Turner. You've been terrific, really. But . . . well . . . stay out of my mess. I mean, you only complicate things."

The engine kicked over after two or three tries. Turner backed out with a cloud of smoke from the exhaust, and headed onto Wilshire. He drove for a while without saying anything. At a stoplight, he looked over at her, in the disheveled dressing gown that she had put on for him the night before.

"Trying to run is crazy," he said gently.

"That's what Jacky says," she agreed with a sigh.

Turner stared at her, ignoring the horns behind him as the light turned green. "Who the hell's Jacky?"

"My hairdresser. The light's green."

The Chevy bucked across the intersection angrily. "You told your *hairdresser?*" He was incredulous.

She indicated the next street coming up. "Turn there, it's the first block on the right. He's also my husband," she explained. "You wouldn't understand—"

"Hey, wait a m—"

"Look. If the cops get their hands on me, they won't go looking for anybody else," she pointed out. "This is the building, stop here."

"Not true," Turner argued. "They—"

"—because of the other time," she cut in quietly.

They had pulled up in front of a lovely old apartment building fighting the good fight against seediness and salt water rot. Alex didn't get out of the car. She just sat there while her words sank in, ready to explain if he wanted it.

"What other time?"

"My ex-husband once called the cops. Had me arrested, and tanked." She said it with no sign of emotion. Whatever had been there in the emotion department was long since eroded and gone.

Turner had swiveled around under the wheel to stare at her in total confusion. "Jacky did?" he asked, trying to sort things out.

"Jacky's not my ex-husband," she explained, being patient with a slow learner. *"Before* Jacky there was another guy. We were kids."

Turner nodded. "Why'd he put you away?"

"Because he was an asshole," Alex snapped. She still made no effort to get out of the car. After a minute, she shrugged and went on, "We'd been sort of discussing our problems over a couple of drinks. It was a weekend." She stopped and waited, but Turner was listening carefully and saying nothing. She didn't like this, but . . . well, he was listening. Maybe she owed him something, even if it was only an explanation. "Next thing I knew . . . he was bleeding." She gestured with her slim index finger, along her left cheek from her ear to the corner of her mouth. "And there I was with a paring knife in my hand."

Turner didn't flinch. "How long were you inside?"

"A while. Three months."

"Long enough to know what it is," Turner said.

There was genuine compassion in his voice; she could hardly believe it. All she could do was nod. Damned right it was long enough. Long enough not to ever want a repeat.

Alex popped open the last of the six-pack.

"I guess you've been drinking for a long time," he said.

She shook her head. "I wasn't really drinking back then. We were—"

"Kids," he cut in. "I know."

She put her hand on the door handle. "You really drink now?" Turner asked her.

Defiant, she answered sharply. "No. When I want. Who the hell's side are you on?" When he didn't say anything, she bit back the hurt. "Thanks," she said.

"Whose place is this?" Turner asked.

"A friend's."

"This one alive?"

She shot him a furious look and started pulling at the door handle. "Maybe you did kill that guy," Turner said.

She turned to him furiously. "I *didn't*." But her anger didn't carry any conviction. She wasn't all that sure.

Chapter
Nine

SHE RATTLED THE DOOR HANDLE, TRYING TO GET OUT OF the car.

"Either you did it and you blacked out . . ." Turner reasoned out loud, with no concern for her feelings, "or you blacked out and were set up."

Alex didn't need this. "I vote for number two," she said. "So long, Turner, nice talking to you." She pushed at the door, which refused to budge.

"Either way," Turner went on, "you're a lush with a record and they'll charge you with murder—"

At the word "lush," Alex grabbed a beer can from the floor and threw it at his head, hard. His right arm went up instinctively to ward it off, but the arm didn't work right and the can struck his forehead, with beer spraying all down his face and shirtfront.

"—what else d'you call somebody who guzzles beer nine o'clock in the morning!" he yelped.

"You bought it for me, you son of a bitch!"

She struggled with the door. The damned thing wouldn't budge. "It's stuck," Turner said. "Y'gotta—"

"I know, I know! Grab it with both hands and shove!" That's what she *had* been doing but this time, maddeningly, it worked. The door whipped open and she damned near fell out. She caught herself by hanging onto the handle and refusing by sheer willpower to fall in the gutter. "Why don't y'get your lousy car fixed?" she shouted at him.

"I don't have the money!" he shouted back, just as mad as she was.

"So get a job, you bum!"

"In the movies? Like you?"

She wanted to kill him. She slammed the door and then reached back through the open window for the second six-pack. She was shouting full-blast all the time: "Asshole! You're great at pushing around adolescent girls, but you can't hack it as a civilian, can you! What's the problem? All the spics and spades and kikes and fags grabbed up the good jobs? Except for the ones on relief, of course! With their Caddies double-parked outside, paid for with your hard-earned tax money! It's a goddamned Commie conspiracy, isn't it?"

He leaned over onto the passenger seat to snarl out the window at her. "Maybe it *is*, yeah!"

"Just no room in the world any more for a good, God-fearing bigot!"

"You're damned right!" Turner's face was beet-red, his eyes blazing with rage.

"Ahhh, shove it up your lily-white ass, Turner." She turned to get away from him.

Turner went wild, struggling with the door. "You foulmouthed bitch drunk!"

"Grab it with both hands and shove!" she advised. She turned and made a dignified exit up the sidewalk, in her disheveled robe, barefoot, flaunting her six-pack. Turner waited until she was inside the vestibule of the building. She heard the Chevy start up and bounce noisily away as she stood jabbing the intercom button.

"Come on, Frankie. Rise and shine," she muttered to herself. She jabbed again and kept her finger on it.

The phone crackled and someone yawned into it. "Huh?"

"It's me. Alex."

"Oh, hi, girl. What's happenin' . . . ?"

Alex put her hand on the door knob. She shouted back into the intercom phone, "Y'gonna let me in?"

"Yeah, sure. What time is it?" He clicked the door open and she went into the cool dark hallway. Frankie lived in the rear, a garden apartment. His door was open and she poked her head inside. The room was dark, heavily furnished in Victorian rebellion against everything that was California. A framed portrait of Oscar Wilde hung over the art-nouveau carved mantelpiece made of real marble which had been imported from somewhere. She heard voices and hesitated at the door.

"Frankie? Are you alone?"

One of the glass-fronted bookcases was open, revealing a television set behind the facade of phony books. The picture showed a large audience of people all jumping up and down to attract the emcee's attention.

"My God, who *are* all these people?" Frankie asked in mock horror. "What's everybody doing up?"

"It's two in the afternoon, Frankie," Alex told him gently. Her eyes were growing accustomed to the gloom. Frankie stood holding onto the doorframe between the bedroom and living room. He was an androgynous figure, now wrapped in a shorty kimono. His eyebrows were fiercely plucked and his dark hair swept back into a longish ducktail. His fingernails were long and painted a kind of murky plum. He was in his thirties, and wiry, with black eyes that knew a great deal more than they told.

"What a night, you should have been there . . ." he started to say with a yawn, and then he looked up from the television screen at Alex. "Or were you?" he added dryly.

"I need some help," she said. She sat down on a horsehair-stuffed sofa.

"Don't we all?" Frankie murmured. He leaned over to turn down the sound, leaving the picture of greed in motion cavorting soundlessly in the background. He came over to her, sat down and helped himself to a can of beer. He popped it and took a deep swallow, then sat back to relax with his head against the velvet upholstery.

"I don't have any time to waste, Frankie. I need clothes, some makeup—"

He peered at her. "—and a dye job," he commented helpfully.

She pulled her slender fingers through her uncombed hair. "Yeah . . ."

"Come on, then." Frankie got up and led the way into his bedroom. One whole wall was closets. He opened two of the doors wide, exhibiting rows of dresses in a wide range of colors and fabrics on padded hangers. There was an interior wall of high-heeled shoes on specially designed shelves.

"Try this end," he suggested. He pulled out several dresses. What wasn't spangled was feathered. "What d'you think?" he asked her.

Alex didn't want to hurt his feelings. "Well, they're kind of . . . I don't know . . . d'you have anything simpler? A little less . . . *less* . . . ?

Not unkindly, Frankie explained, "Honey, I'm a drag queen, not a transvestite. I don't buy no housedresses." He carefully replaced the silver and glittered gowns and started at the other end of the closet, where the darkest colors hung. He searched through several hangers before coming up with a black crepe, draped number. "Now, here's a thing I bought last year for a date at the Bistro . . . he was with the Mafia, *real* sweet, and you'd be surprised how conservative they are . . . your basic black. What d'you think?"

He read her look. "Doesn't do much, huh? It's better on . . . although maybe it's more my type than yours." He put the dresses back in place. He riffled through the hangers thoughtfully. Suddenly he had an inspiration. "Wait a minute, wait a minute!" he exclaimed excitedly. "There's an outfit I bought for Gregory . . ."

"I don't remember Gregory," Alex said.

Frankie was looking through a series of boxes stacked on the shelves. "About your size?" He looked back over his shoulder but she shook her head, no. "Well, he's been gone the limit," Frankie went on. "They don't show for three weeks, they are *out!* It's over." He got his hands on a mauve-colored box without a label, peeked inside and put it back, kept looking. His voice turned nostalgic. "Used to be three days, in the golden years." But Frankie couldn't stay serious or sad for more than a second. "What the hell, tempus fucks it," he went on. "Hah! Here it is." He pulled out another box from the same elegant store. "From Rodeo Drive," he pointed out proudly. "Honey, it was *love.*"

She opened the box. There was a pair of beautifully stitched and tailored linen trousers, in an exquisite shade of apricot. She held them up to herself; the narrowed cuffs came only a little too close to the rug, no problem once she got on a pair of Frankie's sexy stiletto heels. "Frankie, they're perfect," she said. "I'll need a blouse."

She was offered her choice from a vast collection, and chose a lavender silk shirt that mixed unexpectedly and meltingly with the apricot slacks. A thin leather belt wrapped twice around her waist, and the cuffs of the shirt were rolled to just below her elbows. She left it unbuttoned most of the way down.

A comb, a drop or two of Visine and fresh makeup primed her for the outfit. By the time she was dressed, there was no hint of havoc going on inside that svelte, serene, slender movie-star facade. Frankie put a pair of blue-tinted glasses on her elegant nose before saluting her with kisses on both cheeks and sending her out into the glaring sunlight again.

She would have called a cab but she didn't have a destination clearly in mind. Maybe the day after Thanksgiving was easier to get out of town, but she doubted it—didn't the holiday go on for four days or more? Anyway, if they were at her apartment, they probably had armed guards at the airports and bus terminals ordered to shoot to kill if they saw her. From Frankie's apartment, she could walk to the Strip, find a cool quiet bar and do some cool, quiet thinking.

She got as far as the sidewalk when a too-familiar sight almost made her cry out—with joy or dismay, she wasn't sure. There he sat in that disgraceful Chevy, holding a folded handkerchief to his forehead. She went over to him, feeling good in the sexy sandals, the well-cut clothes. She stopped and leaned down to look at him through the passenger window. No blood on the handkerchief; she hadn't cut him badly, if at all, with the beer can.

"Don't tell me it won't start?" she asked with mock solicitude.

Turner looked at her. "I want to help you," he said.

"You want to help *me?* The foulmouthed bitch?"

He nodded thoughtfully. He was being very serious. "Right."

"The spic-lover, the drunk . . . everything you can't stand."

"That's what you are, all right," he agreed.

Suddenly her voice turned hard. "Then what do you want to help me for?" she asked sharply.

He looked at her in surprise. He lowered the handkerchief from his forehead. A tiny little scratch, hardly noticeable. "Because you're innocent," he said.

Her mouth dropped open. "Innocent . . ."

Turner nodded. "I began to think: there was no

body in your shower last night . . . why would you put one there after I left? You're a lush but you're not stupid."

"Flatterer."

"You're more intelligent than I am," he said without an edge. He was simply sincere.

Alex was touched. "Wow," she said with soft sarcasm. "Praise indeed."

He didn't say anything then, and after a minute, she opened the door with a push-me-pull-you action and got into the car. The engine started right up; he revved it and pulled away from the curb. "Somebody in the closet could mean you were set up," he said. "And if you were set up . . . it could be somebody you know. I want you to make a list, okay? A list of everybody you know."

She pursed her lips for a low whistle. Some list that was going to be. A montage of lovers, friends, bartenders, famous movie faces, producers, directors, relatives, plumbers and journalists went past her head in comic fast-action. Her address book would have helped, but in fact it hadn't been updated since God knew when, and in any case it was in the possession of the cops by now. She found a grimy envelope from the gas company in Turner's glove compartment, behind the tape deck. He had a ballpoint pen in there, too, under some spark plugs and a credit card for a company that had been out of business for five years. As he drove, she started to make a list.

Turner stopped at a Tail O' The Pup hotdog stand, parking under a tree at the far end of the lot. She waited in the car while he went to the counter. The envelope was getting crowded with the people in her life.

He came back with a cardboard tray full of hotdogs, french-fries, and diet sodas. She took it from him while he got in under the wheel, and then managed to prop it up on the rickety slope of the dashboard. She handed him the list. Turner took a hotdog and bit into it, then glanced at the first name.

"Who's Legs?" he asked, with his mouth full.

"Legs." She thought about Legs, and there wasn't much to tell. A knockout-looking chorus girl, had to be in her forties by now, and Alex stopped to wonder what Legs could possibly be doing now. She had a bit part in a film Alex had starred in; one morning Legs had come in with her gorgeous face all bruised from the guy she lived with. Alex had gotten the makeup man to fix her up so the director wouldn't notice, and she had taken Legs home with her to save her life for a couple of days until the guy cleared out. The two women had stayed up all night talking and discovering a mutual capacity for vodka stingers. Stayed friends for a while, but Alex hadn't seen her in years. Wonder what became of her. Wonder why she was the first name on the list, come to think of it. "A friend," she told Turner in answer to his question.

"What kind of friend?" Turner persisted. "Eat some lunch."

"Just a friend . . . She had a boyfriend who was into violence. But I haven't seen her in years. Don't even know why I thought of her." The smell of the hot dogs was making her queasy. She took a sip of the soda. Yech.

"She was a drinking buddy of yours?" Turner asked sharply.

"Briefly. A long time ago, Turner."

He looked over at the list again. "And Jay Perlmutter? Who's he?" Turner asked.

"Big agent. Roseanne Kahn, in his office, sends me up for commercials sometimes."

"Travis?"

This was getting really boring. "I forget. Maybe a friend of Frankie's." Turner stared. "Frankie's the guy who lent me these clothes."

Turner nodded slowly. "Then Frankie's . . . uh . . ." He gestured with his wrist, made it go limp.

Disgusted, Alex mocked, "Yeah, he's . . . uh." She repeated his stupid gesture. "Look, you wanted a list, I made a list. But none of these people would do it."

"Oh! You know what's bein' done?"

"No."

"Then how do you know they're not doin' it?"

Miffed, she changed the subject. "I have to call Jacky. He's going to be worried sick. Maybe he can help, he's smart and he knows the people in charge."

"In charge of what?"

"Everything. The world."

Turner was outraged. "He's a hairdresser!"

"That's what he *does*. That's not what he *is!*" she retorted.

He held up the second hot dog but she declined with a shake of her head and he started on it himself. "How long you and Jacky been separated?" he asked after the first bite.

"How do you know we're separated?" she said.

"I was in your apartment, remember? No hairdresser could live there," Turner said with maddening logic.

"Where'd *you* learn interior decoration—Bakersfield Institute of Art?" She took the hot dog from him, bit off a small section of bun where the greasy mustard had not smeared, and handed it back to him with a grimace. "We've been married ten years," she said.

"How long ago'd you separate?"

"Ten years ago," she said.

"Must be lovely, growin' old together." Turner polished off the hot dog, wiped his hands and face on a batch of paper napkins. He started on the frenchfries.

"We gave it a try but it didn't work," Alex said. A thought occurred to her, and she studied Turner for a minute. "You and Jacky are a lot alike that way . . . temperance types. No tolerance for normal people who like a drink now and then . . . Anyway, as soon as we separated we got close."

Turner shook his head and smiled, but he understood. "I guess it happens that way, sometimes."

"I know, it's crazy. But it's not so crazy. He loves me and he cares how I feel . . . how I am. Nobody else does."

Turner looked at her for a long time. "I do," he said.

Chapter
Ten

ALEX DIDN'T KNOW HOW TO HANDLE WHAT HE'D JUST said. Never had any trouble fielding male advances before, but with Turner she felt so damned *ambivalent*—she hated his short-sleeved shirts and his prejudices and yet, there were moments . . . and he said things like that.

She'd deal with it some other time, ignore it for now. What had she been talking about—oh, yes, Jacky. A very special relationship, hard for other people to understand. More than friendship, more than love—a whole lot better than the kind of love that made two people tear each other apart. They loved each other with tolerance and understanding, and damned few demands. Match that in any marriage you ever heard of.

"And I care what happens to him," she went on, as if Turner hadn't said anything at all. "I helped him, when he got started. He was just a—well, you've got a nice name for it. He was young and broke and ambitious to get somewhere and I was already somewhere. God, we looked good together . . . well, we *liked* each other, and we trusted each other, and . . . well, anyway, I put up a chunk of my savings for his first shop. It was the only smart business move I ever made in my life. He was successful right away." She trailed off, remembering.

"So you got married," Turner prompted.

"Yes."

"And then?"

"And then . . . I guess I started *not* getting parts in pictures . . ." It hurt. Then, because Turner was waiting for her to finish, she said, simply, "Jacky takes care of me."

He nodded. "Whose idea is stayin' married?"

"Both of us."

"How come?"

"I think I keep him out of trouble with those Beverly Hills clients he scores. You know—'I love you, babe, but I'm already married' is a great exit line."

"You mean he's straight?" Turner looked dubious as hell.

Well, he was predictable, you could say that for him. Alex let the sarcasm show. "Yes, Turner, there are straight hairdressers."

"In Bakersfield, Jacky's a gay name," he informed her.

"Well, his name is really Joaquin. Manero." And I'll bet I know what you'll make of that one, Turner Smith, she thought.

Turner was on his best behavior. "You married a . . . an Hispanic?"

Alex smiled. "Did me more good than the WASP I tried first." She pushed-pulled the door open and turned to get the tray off the dashboard. As she deposited it in the jumbo trashcan near the hot dog stand, she spotted a phone booth. Instinctively, she reached for her purse, but of course it was back in her apartment. She came back to the car, but instead of getting in, she held out a hand to Turner. "Spare change, Mister?"

He had seen the phone booth, too. Without a word, he dug in his pocket and offered her a handful of change. He kept her covered with his eyes as she sauntered back to make her call. Was anyone paying her any special attention?

The phone didn't have time to complete one ring before it was picked up. "Jacky's."

"Hi, Red, is Jacky there? It's important, I've got to talk to him."

"Hi, Viveca. Sorry, but he's not here. Can I have him get back to you?"

"I . . . can't be reached. I'll have to try him later. When's he coming in?"

"He's got a cut at . . . let me see . . . in an hour from now. He'll be here in an hour, maybe earlier."

"I'll try the car."

"Yeah, that's a good idea. And I'll tell him you'll try again if you don't get him, okay?"

"Yeah. Thanks, Red."

"Have a nice day, Viveca."

"Right. You, too."

She tried the Bentley but no answer. Conscious of

104

Turner's eyes on her, she hung up and headed back to the Chevy.

"Can't find him," she said. "Now what?" She got into the car. As depressed as she had ever been, she probed at a particularly unpleasant thought as if it were a toothache in her brain. "Hey, Turner? They're ripping up my apartment, aren't they? Right now."

He nodded. They looked at each other for a minute and then he said something he'd obviously been wanting to say for a while. The words rushed out fast. "Listen, Viveca, there's a cop I know who's with homicide right here in L.A. . . . ."

"No."

"Maybe he can help," Turner said.

"No cops." Alex wasn't sure of much right this minute, but she was damn sure of that much.

"Just on the phone?" Turner bargained.

Alex shook her head. "Why should I trust some cop—just because he's a pal of yours?"

"I don't know," Turner admitted. He thought about it. Why should she trust Herb Greenbaum? Why did *he* trust him? Greenbaum was just an ordinary sergeant on the L.A.P.D., and Turner didn't know him very well at that. They had worked together once, Greenbaum might not even remember. The case of the Bakersfield boy who'd run away to the big city and got in trouble. Turner had been impressed with the way Greenbaum had handled the case, with compassion and concern as well as sharp police work. He knew his stuff and still cared about people. But he probably wouldn't remember a cop from Bakersfield, and even if he did, an ex-cop from

Bakersfield would not be someone he'd want to renew an acquaintance with. It was just gut instinct that was making Turner think Greenbaum would try to help Alexandra. But how to convince her of that . . .

"He's Jewish," he told her.

"Yeah? He'll bring me some chicken soup?"

"Come on," Turner pleaded. He held out a coin for the phone call. She just stared at it.

"I don't know you," she said slowly.

Turner shrugged. "What's there to know?"

"Well . . . why you're interested in . . . all this trouble, to begin with." She stared at him, trying to see beyond the simple good looks and sincere facade.

"Because it's happening to you," he said simply.

She almost laughed. "All we've done is fight."

Turner allowed himself a little smile, too. "Better than nothin'," he said.

She looked at him but there was no more clue to figuring him out than there had ever been. In fact it was getting harder. She took the coin he was holding out.

"And if I call your friend, and he puts me in the slammer, I suppose you'll come and visit me from time to time. Maybe the two of you?" She was stalling.

"Call him," Turner urged her quietly, not smiling.

She reached for the door handle again but he leaned over to stop her. His hand on her arm was firm, and she yearned to lean on it. Instead she just looked at him quizzically.

"Been here too long," he told her.

She sat back. "I'm beginning to feel depressingly

at home in this Chevy," she commented as he touched off the ignition wires. Turner nodded; he knew just what she meant. They headed out of the area, aimless for a while.

They talked it over. Turner had an idea how Herb Greenbaum might help. He rehearsed Alex in what to say. There was one place in that loft on Mateo Street where there might still be fingerprints—and they wouldn't be hers. All Alex and Turner had to do was stay out of the way till it was over. But first she had to make the call.

"I could use a drink, Turner," Alex said. "How about you?"

Turner nodded. He cruised the edging-on-slum streets in central L.A., looking for a likely, anonymous oasis.

Two men dressed like plainclothes detectives were leaning on the reception desk talking to Red. Jacky breezed in as he always did, on the run toward the stairs, with a smile and a salute to his clients. But one glance and he knew these characters weren't there for a cut and blow-dry. He slowed down.

"Jacky, these two gentlemen have been waiting to see you," Red said redundantly, with a big smile for the one who'd obviously been flirting with her to pass the time a little. He was tall and lean, with a face that was supposed to mislead you with its friendliness. The other cop was older and shorter and balder. "And Viveca called," Red went on. Jacky gestured for her to shut up, but she missed it. ". . . she can't be reached but she'll try again," Red finished lamely as the light dawned, too late.

"Thanks, Red," Jacky said dryly.

"Where's a good place to talk?" the tall cop asked. Jacky led the way upstairs to his private salon. They pulled a couple of chairs around in a three-way circle and parked themselves.

The tall light-haired cop started, pleasantly enough. "Viveca Van Loren's your ex-wife?"

"We're still married, legally," Jacky told him.

"But you don't live together." This was the other man, the rougher type.

"No. We haven't lived together for ten years."

"You know she's in trouble?" asked the first guy, almost solicitously.

"What kind of trouble?" Jacky asked him.

"A corpse turned up in her apartment. Didn't she tell you that when she called?"

"No." Jacky wasn't volunteering anything he didn't have to. He remained cool and unruffled by this information.

"You and she still keep pretty close, huh?" The cops were taking turns asking questions. Instead of turning from one to the other like watching a tennis match, Jacky shoved his chair back to get them both in his scope at once.

"What's this about? I've got people waiting for me . . ."

"Well, looks like your wife killed this guy, a kinky photographer named Bobby Marshack. You ever heard of him?" asked the feisty cop. He looked like an old-timer, probably very good with his fists.

"I think so. He's pretty famous, isn't he?"

"Viveca told you a lot of things, about herself? Her life and her . . . friends? Who she was seeing, stuff like that?"

"No, not much. We went our separate ways."

108

"You know whether she was having something with this guy she killed? This Marshack?"

Jacky permitted himself a scornful laugh. "Come on! Viveca never killed anybody," he protested.

Cop number two leaned forward in his seat with a mean look. "Stiffs just use her apartment to take showers in?" he sneered.

Jacky looked puzzled. "Her shower?"

"That's where we found him," said the good guy, almost apologetically.

"She's not capable of murder. I know her," Jacky insisted.

The mean cop shook his head. "She's got a violent record. Assault with a deadly weapon."

"Did you know that when you married her?" the tall one asked sympathetically. He was leaning forward, too, eager to catch Jacky if he tripped on a question.

"It's *why* I married her," Jacky spat out. "Are you just here passing the time of day or should I call my lawyer?" He stood up. The plainclothes cops had no choice but to follow him out of the private office and onto the balcony overlooking the main salon. Casting a gluttonous look at the women in various stages of work on their hair, faces and bodies, Cop number two commented, "Great spot for a stud." He turned before going down the steps to sneer, "Or are you a fag, Jacky?"

Jacky had heard that a few zillion times before. "How bad do you want to know?" he retorted.

He didn't bother to see them out.

Chapter
Eleven

HER HANDS WERE COLD. HER WHITE FINGERS clenched around the handkerchief Turner had lent her to wipe the heat of the afternoon from her cheeks and forehead. He drove in a crazy pattern, doubling back and circling through shopping malls and freeways.

"Are we being followed? I saw this in the movies." She could still banter, although now that she had agreed to call Turner's cop, all she really felt was scared. Why was she trusting this guy, anyway—just because she couldn't reach Jacky? But Jacky had told her to call the cops, too. So it was the right thing to do . . . but *they* didn't have their lives to lose. Neither Jacky nor Turner had ever been shoved inside with the key turned on them. They hadn't gotten letters from their mothers saying don't ever contact us again, as far as we're concerned you are dead and we are mourning the little girl you were and the fine woman you could have been if you'd only stayed in Illinois . . .

"I'm just being careful," Turner said. He turned onto Sepulveda—not the place to keep a low profile while driving a clunking, belching, thirty-year-old Chevy that didn't know what color it was. Chocolate-brown Mercedes and silver-blue BMW's and red Trans-Ams sleeked by them on all sides. Before she could point out that people were staring at them, he turned off onto a quiet residential avenue lined with tall palms. She had a feeling the maids were running to the windows as they approached, peering out from behind the drapes to see what was making all that noise.

Finally they turned into a suburban neighborhood mall. Nothing fancy: two shoe stores, a superdrug, 24-hour grocery, a Chinese restaurant and a bar. He parked near the drugstore. She led the way into the cool dark pub, cozily old-fashioned Irish. Only two solitaries, neither of whom turned around to notice them. One had a T-shirt with a lengthy slogan on the back: *The Lord invented whiskey to keep the Irish from taking over the world.* The other, down at the end of the bar, was a woman, making circles on the polished wood with her glass and humming along with the rock pap on the radio.

"Vodka with soda on the side," Alex told the bartender.

"Coke," Turner ordered.

"Make it a double," Alex called out in a flash of anger. Who the hell was he to play holier than thou; why couldn't the jerk unbend and have a drink with her, be a little human? He wasn't her judge; she hadn't elected him.

Turner paid for the drinks and nursed his coke until she had downed the vodka. They didn't talk. She felt the blood coursing through her again, and she was ready. Call the cops, the only thing to do. Can't keep running, live in that old Chevy forever. Turner had a friend. Turner trusted his friend and she trusted Turner. Didn't she?

"Okay," she said. "Let's go."

There was a phone booth at the edge of the parking area. Turner got in the car and waited, watching her and sweeping the whole area with his eyes as she made the call.

The desk cop had a patient, calm, middle-aged voice. "Los Angeles Police Department."

She cleared her throat. The cop waited. Finally she took control of her voice, and in a tone only a little higher than normal, asked to speak to Sergeant Herbert Greenbaum.

"Sergeant Greenbaum." A nice strong voice. She'd bet he jogged at least five miles every morning.

"A . . . a friend of yours said I should call," she told him. She'd never been this nervous in her life. She tried to push away the surge of memories—cops sneering and pawing at her, the female guard who liked to start fights among the inmates, the humiliation of—push it away. This cop was going to help her. Ho ho.

"Yeah." Greenbaum sounded bored. She didn't think she could go through with it; she thought about just hanging up, and somehow convincing Turner to take her away, someplace, anyplace, just the hell out of L.A.

"Yeah?" Greenbaum repeated, sounding more interested. Her silence was making him curious. "Hello?" he said again.

Alex hesitated. She had to say something or he'd hang up, and she wasn't sure she'd ever get up the nerve to call him back. But she couldn't say what she had to. "What're you doing in the L.A.P.D. with a name like Greenbaum?" was what finally came out.

Greenbaum was only mildly irked. "Is that the purpose of your call, ma'am? This is some kind of survey? You with the B'nai B'rith?"

She didn't say anything. Maybe if he kept talking, she'd find the nerve to tell him what she had to tell him. Keep talking, Greenbaum, you're a sketch, she thought as she listened to him.

Her silence this time seemed to interest him enough to give her a straighter answer. "My mother was Irish," he said. "Will that make it easier to talk?" Maybe he was thinking that they'd play a game of Truth; first he'd confess something about himself and then she would. Confess something. Listening to his voice turn nicer, she thought maybe he wasn't so dumb; it might work. But she had nothing to confess to. Not yet, but you're getting warm, Greenbaum, she thought. "It helps *me*," Greenbaum went on, sincere as hell.

She took a deep, deep breath. "I'm calling about a body." Her hands clutched the phone so hard her fingers ached.

Greenbaum took it in stride. "Any particular body?" he asked carefully.

Alex cleared her throat. "Uh . . . the one you found at 1560 Laurel . . . a Mister Marshack?"

"Oh, that one," Greenbaum said. "Yeah . . ."

He sounded a bit distracted, as if he were signaling to someone else while talking to her. Keenly interested now, yet distracted. Suddenly she could picture him and what he was doing. "Your friend doesn't want you to trace this call," she told him boldly.

"What about Marshack?" Greenbaum wanted to know. She didn't answer. "Hello?" Alex stood there gripping the phone and staring over at the inviting sign on Madden's Pub: Happy Hour 5–7. "Are you Viveca Van Loren?" Greenbaum asked suddenly.

"I didn't do it!" Alex blurted out.

Greenbaum was quick to answer, in a calm and soothing voice that she wanted very much to trust. "I'd really like to hear your side of it, Viveca. Maybe we—"

"I just thought you should know that where he wound up isn't . . . where he started. So to speak," she trailed off limply. The perspiration was pouring in rivulets down her face.

"So to speak?" Greenbaum echoed, encouragingly.

"I mean if I tell you *where* it happened maybe you can find out *how* it happened." Alex looked out the steamy, stained window of the phone booth toward the Chevy. Turner was sitting there, his eye on her, steady and strong. She hoped she was doing the right thing.

"You're giving me a clue?" Greenbaum asked.

"An address," she agreed. "I'll give you an address. D'you have a pencil?"

"I had one . . . it's got to be here someplace . . . you know, I always wanted to meet you, Viveca . . ."

How long did it take to trace a call, she wondered. He was stalling, she knew that much. "You find the pencil?" she asked sharply. Cut the crap, Greenbaum, was what she meant.

He got the message. "Right here," he answered quickly.

"He was killed in a loft apartment . . . on Mateo Street. 544 Mateo Street. Look inside a closet right inside the door of the apartment. I think you'll find the killer's fingerprints inside that closet. *Inside*. That's it. Okay, Sergeant?"

"Call me Herbie," Greenbaum said.

"If you want to be my friend, Herbie, go right over there," Alex said urgently. She watched Turner get out of the Chevy and start toward her.

"I do want to be your friend, Viveca," Greenbaum said earnestly. "Listen, a movie star—when does a policeman get a chance to meet a movie star?"

"When she's in trouble," Alex answered. "Are you going over there, Herbie? Or are you just interested in getting me to hold onto this phone until you can get your boys over here—"

"Listen, Viveca, who's the friend recommended me to you?" Greenbaum wanted to know. But Turner was at the booth, pushing open the door. He reached inside and broke the connection.

"Time to get off the street," he said. "C'mon."

She followed him with long strides back to the Chevy. It was like climbing into a blast furnace.

As he drove, Alex told him about the conversation with Greenbaum. "Do you think he'll check out Mateo Street?" she asked.

Turner peered into the rearview mirror. Nobody behind them. They were heading for downtown by way of a jungle of side streets nobody ever heard of, some only a block or two long. "Can't tell," Turner said. "Depends on what else they've got. Only Herb's got real sense and . . . yeah, I think so."

She was jumpy, couldn't sit still. It was so goddamned *hot*. "Where we heading?" she asked. Probably nowhere. Maybe this was her sentence—to spend the next ten to twenty years riding around in this goddamned Chevy with the noise and the smell and no hint of air-conditioning.

Turner suddenly swung the car into an alley. They were a couple blocks off Vermont, parallel to it. The engine grumbled to a stop and died. "My place," Turner said. He seemed almost shy, the way he had at dinner on the patio at her apartment all those years ago, last night. Kind of sweet. He got out of the car and, uncharacteristically, came around to open the passenger door for her.

"I didn't know people lived here," she said, getting out and looking around at the grungy utilitarian alley. Mostly garbage cans, bent out of shape and on their sides. These were the back entrances and loading doors for butcher shops and dry cleaners, family grocery stores and God-knew-what that lined the street. The buildings were two and three stories high, and washing was hanging on a line strung across the alleyway overhead. It smelled wretched.

"People live in back of the stores," Turner said. He led the way to an inconspicuous door with no sign or number visible, and unlocked it. "Maybe I should go in first and turn on some lights," he said.

Alex peered past him into the pitch-dark interior. No light at all seeped in through the small, barred windows. From the alley, they looked as though they had been painted black.

She waited out there while he went inside. After a minute, a low-watt bulb sent a subtle beacon out from the front room, which was a kitchen on the left and on the right a kind of dining room/used book emporium. The kitchen area was sparkling clean and an eclectic collection of copper-bottom pans hung on the walls. Small appliances were neatly pigeonholed into a special wall unit from which hung scores of cooking utensils of every description. The area was small but well-designed, with a butcher-block counter and customized stove, sink and refrigerator. The other part of the front room was less organized— books everywhere, some still in boxes, and sparse furnishings. In lieu of a dining table, there was a workbench on which various small appliances and gadgets waited in various stages of repair. The place needed a lighting expert—almost no daylight filtered in through the high barred windows, and the lamps had never been intended to illuminate an entire room. The result was pockets of light suitable for reading, but not much else.

Turner seemed nervous. She guessed that he hadn't shown this place to many people. "I only came to L.A. a while ago, with my wife," he told her, although she hadn't asked. ". . . a month after that we got divorced. She went back . . . we split up the stuff." He seemed to need to explain, and he was a little embarrassed, not used to talking about his personal life.

"Everybody gets divorced," Alex said.

Turner shook his head. "I don't believe in divorce," he told her.

"Don't *believe* in it?" she repeated incredulously. He was weird sometimes.

"I mean I hate it," Turner explained tersely.

Alex shrugged. "Why'd you do it?"

"*She* did. She said I wasn't . . . promising."

Alex felt an inexplicable surge of sympathy. She knew how that felt. Deliberately, she deflected her feelings. This was no time in her life to get soft on a goddamned ex-cop. She looked around the impressive kitchen. "Well, she left you all her cookery stuff," she commented.

"That was mine," Turner said.

"He cooks, too! You're a real find. She must have been crazy," Alex said, only half sarcastic.

"I don't know," Turner told her. "I see her point."

Alex looked at him. "Don't you lie about *anything,* Turner?"

"Sure," he said. Then, contradicting himself, he added, "What's worth lying about?"

She smiled, a little sadly. "How about showing me the rest of the place?" she asked him. He led her through the narrow rooms, switching on lights as they moved into the living room (one chair, coffee table, stacks of books everywhere), bedroom (mattress and springs on the floor, neatly folded blanket and two clean pillows, reading light, more books), and bathroom (the usual, clean and tidy).

"You're a great reader, huh?" she commented.

He was getting more shy by the minute. "These?" he said. "Yeah, well . . . Nah. I mean, I plan to read them, when I have the time, y'know?" He led the way back to the front of the apartment. Alex moved around, picking up books at random, looking at the titles and thumbing through now and then, while he explained. "I just buy books. Quarter a piece, sometimes, in Santa Monica. Or even by the pound. I can't resist. All the subjects interest me." He grinned at her. "I'll get to 'em," he said.

"So what's keeping you so busy?" she asked.

He was still smiling, kind of sheepishly. "You know. Nothin'. Daily life."

Alex nodded. "That'll do it. Daily life."

Her hands moved over the rows and stacks of books. Suddenly she spotted something wonderful. "My God! Nancy Drew . . . a complete set!" she exclaimed.

"I'm saving them for my kid. Only . . . now she just told me she's too old for them," Turner said.

"Too old?" Alex sighed. She pulled out one of the books and said, with absolute honesty and a large dollop of nostalgia, "I always loved her." She wanted to repeat the name; it evoked such innocent, good days. Reading on the window seat with an apple, after school. "Nancy Drew," she said dreamily. "She's so . . . healthy and smart and . . . enthusiastic . . ."

Watching her, Turner was struck by a chord he'd never expected to find in her. The actress was shorn away and underneath there was a lovely, pure—

yes, pure —young girl with fantasies and dreams of being—well . . . healthy and smart . . . and enthusiastic . . .

"Would you like them?" he asked her.

"What?"

"You can have 'em if you like."

"Oh . . . no, I couldn't . . ."

"Why not?"

"No . . . really . . ."

"Please."

". . . Are you sure?"

"Positive."

". . . All right . . ."

"Good." Turner smiled happily.

It seemed to Alex that no one had ever given her anything with so much meaning. She felt kind of choked up, sentimental, even. "I would love them," she said, with a pale smile, remembering where she was and why. "When I'm in the clear."

Turner nodded. "When you're in the clear," he agreed.

She sat down on the arm of the couch. Suddenly she was crying, quietly, without a sound.

"It's been a long one, uh?" Turner said sympathetically. He turned away, giving her privacy.

The crying was brief, and when it subsided she wiped her eyes. "What do we do now?" she asked.

"Wait," Turner said. "Just wait for Greenbaum to do his job."

"Waiting for Greenbaum," Alex sniffed. "I think I saw the play."

He came over to her, and for a minute she thought he was surely going to put his arms around her, but he didn't.

120

"You're a rare dame, Viveca," he said.

"Don't call me a dame, Turner." She smiled a little. " 'Rare' I like, though."

There was something happening now, something maybe overdue, but now suddenly it was in the air between them, impossible to ignore.

Chapter Twelve

"LISTEN," ALEX SAID. SHE DIDN'T TAKE HER EYES from his. "Viveca's my fake name. I'm really Alex Sternbergen."

He nodded thoughtfully. "Were you ever a sports announcer, out of Cincinnati?"

"Alex for Alexandra," she told him.

"Ah. Nice."

"I like it, too," she said. "Like when you're having an argument, it's not so easy to *yell* 'Alexandra.'"

"So . . . would it bother you if I called you 'Alexandra'?" he asked, like a kid wondering if he could have a special treat.

"If you promise not to yell it," she told him.

He studied her, very closely, and then he promised. "No. I won't yell it."

He took her hand. Alex nodded. It was time.

Then, with a surprising, sweet sort of urgency, she said, "You got anything to drink?"

Turner nodded. "Little vodka," he said. "You want some?"

Alex shook her head. "No," she said.

They stood there for a while, savoring being close, knowing what was going to happen, not in a hurry. It felt awfully good. "What's going on, Turner?" she asked him. "Do you know?"

"I'll check that loft tomorrow, see if—"

"Here, I mean. Now."

". . . Yeah. I know."

"What is it? We want to get laid?" she asked.

Turner shook his head, not giving up her hand. "Why do you do that?" he asked.

"What?" she said, but he had her number. Why was she deliberately trying to spoil it? Why did she always spoil everything?

"You haven't wanted to get laid in years," Turner told her. She laughed. "I didn't say you *haven't* been," he said. "You just haven't *wanted* it. In years."

Alex was puzzled. "Then why do I feel—"

She took her hand out of his, and looked down at it. Turner hesitated for the briefest instant, before he moved his face close to hers and lifted her chin and looked at her tenderly and then kissed her. Caught up in desire and longing and an attraction she couldn't fathom, she kissed him back.

His lovemaking was tender but not tentative, and she found herself responding to his caresses and kisses with a passion she hadn't felt in a very long time. How did he know so much about her, about her inner feelings and her body, her needs and pleasures? She felt him *caring* about her all through his movements and his words. She found him exciting and beautiful and deeply satisfying in every move he made. Every endearment he uttered she believed.

Sometime in the middle of the night, she raised herself on an elbow and traced one finger across the tiny scrape on his forehead where she'd beaned him with the beercan. She put her lips against it, to make it all better. Then she moved her hand slowly down along his cheek, his chin and the strong lines of his throat to his shoulder—where she found another scar. It was deep and had been heavily stitched. Drowsily, she moved her hand over it, soothing, wishing it away.

He sighed and leaned up to kiss her.

"Stay till morning?" she murmured without thinking.

"Sure," Turner said. He kissed her again, longer. "I live here," he said.

She started to laugh, but he kept on kissing her. She reached her arms around to hold him tightly, in a deep embrace that had the power to ward off the world forever, or at least for a while.

He made love the second time as if there were still an infinite amount of discovering to do. His wonderment and the joy he took in her made Alex feel special somehow—like a first time, despite everything. He fell asleep still holding her close. She lay awake for a while, savoring contentment, pleased to be part of his regular rhythmic breathing.

After a while her arm started to ache from being too long in one position. She eased it away from his neck, stretched it across the pillow. In his sleep, Turner murmured something indistinguishable, and he stirred a bit, then slowly turned away. Alex lay beside him, wide awake. Her legs began to cramp and she didn't want to toss around, possibly waking him. She got up carefully and stood naked in the shaded lamplight, watching him sleep.

She was filled with wonder, both the awe kind and the asking kind. Wonder at such tenderness and such masculine beauty; wondering who he really was, how he got that way, how she could please him, how long before he lost patience with her.

She was afraid of what had happened between them. She had been staying far away from intimacy with a man for a very long time. One night stands were okay—they only made you feel dirty and disgusted; at least you didn't get hurt. Caring for someone only led to disappointment and hurt. Better to stay flip and cool, unreachable . . . How long, she wondered again, how long?

She turned and went into the kitchen. It took some rummaging around, but she found a bottle of vodka. She sat down with it at the kitchen table.

She was still there when daylight turned the dark apartment to a grudging gray. She hadn't moved by the time Turner woke up and came to find her. He bent and kissed her. "Good morning," he said. "Couldn't sleep?"

She didn't answer. The vodka was nearly all used up.

Turner went back to the bedroom and damn-all if she didn't hear him whistling. Then the shower. Pretty soon he came back to the front of the apartment all spiffed up in another truly awful shirt. "I'm going out to get some breakfast stuff," he told her. "Back in a few minutes. You okay?"

She nodded. Fine. Really swell, terrific.

He went out the kitchen door, which was the only door, and she just stayed right there where it was cozy. She worked on the vodka.

He came back with some fresh bread and butter and jam and the *Los Angeles Times*. He propped the newspaper up on the table, and then started brewing up a large pot of coffee. He squeezed some oranges and put a loathsome glass of juice in front of her.

"Don't you drink?" she asked him belligerently. Never trust people who don't drink. They'll turn on you every time.

He didn't answer. He was standing at the toaster waiting for the stuff to pop up, and he was thinking, she could tell. Thinking about her predicament. Well, so was she. The vodka was almost gone.

She looked at the *Times*. Picture of herself on the front page. PHOTOG MURDERED, ACTRESS SOUGHT. Under that, in only slightly smaller print, it said: VIVECA VAN LOREN HAS SLASHER HISTORY. The picture had been taken a long, long time before—during her studio days. It was airbrushed beyond recognition, but she sure did look good. She read through the story as well as she could, although the ink seemed to be a little blurred.

"You'd think they'd mention the one good movie I made!" she bitched. She pushed the paper aside, and it fell to the floor. Turner buttered a piece of toast and put it next to the juice before her. The coffee steamed up from a huge mug under her nose.

"I went by Martineau's," Turner said. He picked

up the newspaper from the floor and sat down across from her. "That place you said you were at? Marshack was never there."

Alex thought about that for a while and finally the implications sank in. "Then where'd I meet him?" she asked.

"You don't know?"

"No." Trying to be absolutely accurate, she amended the statement. "Yeah. In bed," she said.

Turner didn't like her this morning; she could tell. Well, better sooner than later . . . or something like that. He didn't like what she just said, she knew that. But he was being super-detective and very, very serious this morning. Solve the case, that was the ticket. First things first. She was glad he was that way. He was solving her case, wasn't that nice? She was really lucky to have him on her side.

"You made a phone call at Martineau's," he told her. "Also, you got a phone call there that night."

He waited. Nothing. "Well?" he asked.

She was trying to remember. Yes, Martineau's . . . she had been meeting someone there, a business appointment, a casting director. But she couldn't remember going into the club, sitting down —where had she sat? Faces? No. Nothing. She shook her head.

"Nothing?" Turner asked.

"No," she told him sadly.

"Y'remember last night?" Turner asked abruptly.

She looked up then and met his gaze with a long, level look. "Yes," she said.

He considered that, for a moment, and then went back to business. She could hardly see over the wall between them now. How did it get there, probably her fault. Definitely her fault. Damn . . . but there was still something nice on the other side. Turner was *nice*. She had to be on her guard against nice guys, they always turn out badly.

"I was thinking," Turner said, "maybe somebody asked you to leave? On the phone?"

She searched her head but there was no memory of anything like that.

Turner got up and took some dishes to the kitchen sink. She watched him for a moment. His back was turned to her. Suddenly she found herself on the edge of self-pity.

"Why'd they pick me, Turner?" Her speech was slurred, almost a whine.

She had tapped into his own anger. He turned to her. "Why *not*? You're perfect for it. You've got a record . . . and you're a blackout drunk! Working your way down. You've already pissed away half your life!"

Alex hit back instinctively. "You made such a hit out of yours? Restoring toasters!"

She shoved the plate with her untouched toast off the table. It crashed on the floor. Turner ignored her. He was at the sink again.

She watched the muscles move in his arms as he washed the dishes and stacked them neatly on the rack. After a while, she said wretchedly, "See . . . you don't know what it's like."

"What?" he asked coldly, not turning around.

"Losing it," she said. "What'd you ever have?"

He didn't answer.

"I was an actress," she told him, with something of the inflection of her long-ago teacher Althea.

Pride, Althea had said, makes your voice heard beyond the second row. If you haven't got it, don't try to become an Actor. "I was an Actress," she repeated proudly.

He whirled around. "You drink, Alexandra! Fucking booze!"

"You're yelling!"

She poured a little more vodka into her glass. In an instant, he was across the room, his arm raised. He knocked the glass out of her hand and onto the floor. The vodka spilled out and the shards of glass flew all over the place. "Don't you want to know what's going on?"

She looked down at the broken glass with the vodka spilling out onto the linoleum, mixing with the toast and broken china plate. Turner reached for a dustpan and knelt down to sweep it up. He dumped the mess into the garbage can and then brought her another glass. He emptied the bottle into it. Alex watched him. Then, almost sweetly, she said, "That's not the problem. A little vodka."

Turner nodded. "I know. It's the pain."

"It's the pain," she agreed.

"Like nobody's got any but you."

"What do you know about it?" Suddenly Alex couldn't sit there another minute. The place was getting to her, and so was he, and the crowding-in of everything in her life . . . talking about pain . . . "I want to get out of here!" she moaned urgently.

"And go where?" Turner asked.

Well, that was an unfair question. She hadn't had time to think about that one. And anyway, she had a hell of a buzz on. There was somebody who might be able to help her, she remembered dimly. Somebody she was counting on . . . sure! Turner's old buddy, a cop. That's who.

"Where's Greenberg live?" she demanded.

"Greenbaum."

"They live together? That's sweet," Alex said. She stood up, unsteadily, and was trying to move toward the door. Turner kept getting in the way.

"Look," Turner said, nicely. "Will you do something for me?"

She considered. What a nice face he had. He had loved her last night, really loved her, for a little while. "Have I ever denied you anything?" she asked sturdily.

"Stay here," Turner said. "Take a nice long shower. Put your clothes on. I'll be back. Okay?"

She looked at herself and giggled. Naked as a jaybird. "Okay," she said. She tried to salute but her hand waggled through her hair instead of wherever it was supposed to go. She'd wash her hair, too, really surprise him.

But by the time she stepped out of the shower she was reasonably sober again, and had some ideas of her own. She found an iron that worked and pressed Frankie's shirt and trousers neatly, the way her mother had taught her. She used Turner's comb and toothbrush, left him a note, and walked out into the garbage-lined alley. It was time she stopped playing scared little girl and started taking her life in her own hands.

Chapter
Thirteen

ALEX HAD RUMMAGED THROUGH THE POCKETS OF EVERY pair of jeans and both jackets hanging in Turner's closet. She found several bills and some change, enough for a taxi to Beverly Hills, she hoped. She'd pay him back.

The cab pulled up at an ivy-crowned three-story building on North Rodeo Drive. She walked into the atrium entrance, checked her appearance in the reflection of one of the discreet professional plates glinting in the sun. It was a building that housed only law firms, one to a floor. She looked fine, but she'd keep the sunglasses on; they covered a sleepless night.

She was waiting for the elevator when a long black Lincoln glided to a stop out front. A man in his sixties, trim and tanned, stepped out without waiting for his driver to open the door for him. He was carrying an attaché case and an overnighter; his stride was that of a man eager to pit himself against whatever the day had to offer. Alex put on a great big smile and waited for him to come into the lobby.

"Ted!" she exclaimed. "I'm just on my way to see you."

"Viveca, what a lovely sight you are," Ted Harley responded warmly. He kissed her cheek.

The doors to the glass elevator opened, and they stepped inside. At the third floor, they walked toward the double doors to his penthouse suite offices in silence. She waited for him to say something. Either he was being super-discreet or he wanted her to bring it up first. But he was carrying an overnight bag, maybe he didn't know.

"You've been out of town?" she asked.

Ted Harley nodded. "Just got off the plane."

"Then you haven't had a chance to read today's paper," she said.

"No. Why?"

They reached the doors to his office: HARLEY & HIRSCH. Ted shepherded her inside. "Welcome back, Mr. Harley," the receptionist said, all smiles. He nodded a greeting and dropped an envelope bulging with expense receipts on her desk without stopping as he headed for his own office door.

"Messages can wait, Miss Rose," he said. He motioned for Alex to come with him.

Inside the large, book-lined office, with windows looking out onto a private tree-shaded terrace, Alex settled herself in a comfortable leather chair facing the desk. Ted Harley tossed his bag into a closet, came over to the desk and sat down opposite her.

Alex tried to think how to begin. Well, I woke up

with this corpse . . . it was damned difficult. But Ted started talking first. "Jacky reached me in Tokyo," he said. She must have looked very surprised, because Ted smiled and explained, "It's about 88 hours time difference, but you know Jacky when he wants to do something . . ."

"He told you . . . ?"

Harley was a bit confused by her question. "But . . . I assumed he'd already spoken to you."

"Spoken to me?" Alex repeated dumbly.

He looked at her with quickened interest. "Isn't that why you're here?"

"Why?" she echoed.

"We worked it out together, he and I, before I left for Tokyo last Monday," Ted explained. He was trying to read her response, which was hard to do since she felt numb and unable to move a muscle. She just kept repeating words he said.

"Monday?"

Ted looked sympathetic. "Don't you want me to handle it?" he asked her.

It was starting to dawn now. She pushed it away but it kept coming back all the same, making a terrible kind of sense that she didn't want to deal with. She forced herself to stay calm. "Wait . . ." she said. She needed a minute to sort it out, to realize that he was talking about a different problem than the one that was pressing on her.

But Ted Harley kept talking, in his nicest professional bedside manner. "It's simply a matter of formalizing what's been the de facto truth between the two of you for some while . . ." He trailed off.

"What is there to . . . handle?" she asked gingerly.

133

"The divorce," Ted Harley's voice came from a long distance away. She felt faint, but recovered immediately. Damn him. "What else?" Ted was asking.

"Nothing else," she managed to say.

She felt like she'd been hit by the heavyweight champion of the world, with a right and then a left. Wham—you're on the lam for a murder you can't remember whether you did or not . . . bam—oh, by the way, Jacky wants a divorce and hasn't bothered to tell you . . . she wanted to lie down and take the count, but she knew she wouldn't. She was a fighter, too, even when she didn't want to bother any more. She always had been and she always would be. She could take it; she had no choice.

Somehow she managed to say a civil goodbye to Ted and move on out of his office and down the elevator and out onto the street and find that she was still on her own two feet. Way to go, Alex, she groaned. She walked to Wilshire and the few blocks across the tracks to Harry's Bar and Grill, where her credit was good.

An hour later, Alex walked into Jacky's. It was a risk; they were probably watching the place, but she was an actress and even with limited accessories she could change her appearance enough to take a chance. Her hair was completely covered by a kerchief and her dark glasses were large enough to cover the top half of her face. She wore no lipstick and no one would be able to identify her by Frankie's clothes. She *had* to see Jacky. She walked past Red, who would have stopped her if the phone hadn't been ringing off the hook. She went on up the stairs to the mezzanine.

He was standing behind a tall, slender young woman, working with great care and concentration. The haircut would be perfect, worth the large amount of money it cost. The young woman was watching him intently in the mirror. The seriousness with which they were contemplating her hair would have perhaps been more appropriate in an operating room. An assistant stood at Jacky's side, ready to hand him instruments as he reached for them: brush, comb, razor, scissors, all in good time. As Alex reached the top of the stairs, Jacky recognized her in the mirror. Without breaking the mood, he nodded to his assistant and handed her the comb.

"All right, now, would you please take her in for the wash and rinse, Carol? The end cubicle." The client looked upset, but Jacky soothed her quickly. "I'll look in on you. Just a few minutes."

As Carol led the young woman down to the far end of the mezzanine, Jacky moved to head Alex off at the top of the stairs. "Where've you *been?*" he whispered anxiously. He took her arm to escort her into his office.

As soon as they were alone, Alex said abruptly, "Change my looks, will you?"

He stared at her. "It's a mistake," he said. "Whatever you're doing, this isn't going to help."

She pulled off the kerchief and draped it on a towel hook. She made herself comfortable in the chair. Jacky sighed, and came over behind her. He picked up a pair of scissors. They both contemplated her reflection in the mirror.

"What about color?" Jacky asked.

She thought. What would be really different from the way she was known to the world? ". . . Natural?" she suggested.

Jacky examined her hair, holding one long smooth strand between his fingers. He took a comb from the sterilizer and cut a new part, looking at the roots. "Gimme a hint," he said.

"Some kind of brown?"

He nodded, and turned to his long shelf of dyes, rinses, conditioners, magic potions, all with the "Jacky" label on them. He selected two bottles and then a third, and turned back to her. She was looking at him sadly, with all the feelings she hadn't been able to express yet.

"What?" he asked, with concern. "What is it, babe?" He came over to her, put down the bottles and stroked her hair. He looked at her directly, not through the mirror.

"Come on, Jacky," she told him unsteadily. "I . . . talked to Ted Harley. He must've called you."

Jacky nodded. "But you don't understand . . ."

"Yes, I do," Alex said with a small, tight smile. "That's what's so sad. It's not even because of the jam I'm in. He said you talked about it a week ago."

Jacky nodded. His touch on her head became more professional, and he moved around to the back of the chair to begin his work. He combed and said, "That's right. We did."

"You could've come to me first, couldn't you?" she asked bitterly. She almost laughed. "We never even had a fight and you have to go to a fucking lawyer!"

"He's your lawyer too, Alex."

"Was," Alex retorted. "You're the one with all the business now."

"It's just legal shit!" Jacky exploded. He gestured toward the door, the mezzanine outside, the entire shop. "I'm goin' public. You know what that is?"

"Selling stock," she answered. "So?"

"Well, it gets complicated," he said. He swung her around, lowered the chair until the neck-rest was level with the sink that appeared when he touched a button under the work counter. He shampooed her himself, a luxurious treat that he had not performed for anyone in years.

"It's not so complicated," Alex said finally. He didn't answer. "You met somebody, didn't you?" she asked. He was still silent, massaging her scalp, pouring on a cool rinse, and then working warm water through her long thick mane. "Anybody I know?" she persisted.

He shook his head, no. The shampoo was finished, and he wrapped her hair in a towel, brought the chair up to face the mirror again. She watched him in the mirror as he combed through her hair, caressing with one hand and juggling three combs of different sizes and shapes in the other. Say goodbye to being a blonde and having more fun, she told her image silently.

She caught his eye in the mirror. She was still waiting for an answer. He tilted his chin up. "Isabel Harding," he said.

Alex's jaw dropped. "You're kidding."

There was a resentful edge to his answer. "No."

"Harding . . . you mean as in Pasadena?"

"Bel Air," Jacky corrected. Hardings owned most of Pasadena, as everybody knew, but they wouldn't be caught living there. Levelly, he added, "I love her anyway, Alex."

"In spite of her money."

"That's right."

He held her damp hair out to the sides, letting it fall, prompting it in different ways. He brushed it softly until it lay the way he wanted it. He began to cut, ever so delicately, molding her head subtly into a new shape. There was a long silence while they both watched the slow, artful transformation. "She's a client?" Alex asked.

Jacky nodded. There was something about Jacky that was different from the man she had known for so long . . . he had changed. Now she realized what it was—he wasn't playing. She tried to put it together.

"You sometimes do her at home?" she guessed.

"Once in a while."

"Beautiful place?"

"Beautiful enough, yeah," he said.

"And all that money," Alex said.

She'd hit a nerve. "I've *got* money!" Jacky said defiantly.

Alex nodded. She watched his hands, steady and sure, sculpting her head. "But with Harding there's more," she said. "Is it breeding? Is that it? All that Early American stuff . . ."

He didn't answer. She watched him work. "Sure, Jacky," she said finally. "You've been on the outside long enough. It's natural—you want in."

Jacky nodded. "I want in," he agreed.

"Joaquin Manero," she said, making it sound like music.

"You damn right," Jacky said.

"And you won't mind being bored to death?" she asked.

"Not a bit."

Alex nodded. After a moment, she said, "She's probably no more boring than the rest of us."

Jacky grinned. "Yeah, she is," he said.

They laughed together. It was, for a moment, the way it always had been between them.

Chapter
Fourteen

TURNER RANG THE BELL OF THE GROUND-FLOOR FRONT
apartment. The alacrity with which the door was
opened—on the chain—made him think Mrs. James
had probably been watching the street from behind
her chintz curtains, had watched him park the Chevy
across the street and down a few yards, had sized
him up as he approached number 544. She looked
like a woman who didn't miss much—all to the good,
he hoped.

"Good morning. Mrs. James?"

"Yes." She had bright bird's eyes above the reading glasses perched at the end of her longish nose.
She was a spry seventy, he guessed, keen and a bit
suspicious. And honest, he would bet his cop's
instinct on that. A good witness—if she'd seen
anything.

"I'm a private investigator, my name's Turner."
There was no need to spell out the whole thing. That

much was true, and if there was no license for a P.I. with the last name of Turner, there sure as hell wasn't one for Turner Smith, either. But she took his word for it. She stood in the doorway and waited for him to explain what he wanted, ready to slam it shut if he did anything suspicious. He had the feeling this tall, angular woman was all muscle and would be a match for anyone with less than honorable intentions. She peered over the chain at him.

"I'm inquiring about the events of Wednesday night—" he began, but she cut him off.

"I already told everything to the police," she said. She wasn't impatient, only curious.

"I have a picture that I'd like to show you. All right?" He waited for her nod before reaching into his pocket. An elderly lady alone in a neighborhood like this might have mace or God knows what in her hand when she opened the door to a stranger. But she reached through the doorway for the photo, and he handed it to her.

"That's her. That's the one I saw come in that night."

"You're sure?" Turner asked. He took back the photo.

The tall woman pinched her lips together and nodded curtly. "Yes," she said. Then she backtracked a bit. "Well, not to swear in court," she said. "Look at the bulbs he puts in his hallways. Forty watts. He must save fifteen, twenty cents a year keeping us in the dark—"

"What was she doing?" Turner cut in.

"The blonde? Threatening somebody."

Turner didn't much like the answers he was getting, but he plowed on. "Was she armed?"

Mrs. James thought hard, maybe trying to impress him. "I didn't see any weapon," she said finally.

"What was she threatening to do?"

"Well . . . it was more ranting and raving."

"She was drunk?" Turner asked.

Mrs. James had to think again. "I wouldn't say . . . but she could have been," she hedged.

Turner nodded and reached through the narrow opening to shake her hand. She hesitated a second and then took his hand with her strong bony fingers and pressed briefly. "Well, thank you," he said. As if it were an afterthought, he turned back just before she started to shut the door. "Oh . . . had you ever seen her before? I mean, did she visit that second floor apartment often?" he asked.

She shook her head firmly. "Not to my knowledge. That's how I put it to the police," she said, clearly proud of her grip on legal jargon.

Turner nodded. "Thank you." He turned away, and Mrs. James started to close her door. Something moved in the corner of the hall. Turner swiveled quickly and his hand reflexively went for the holster that wasn't there any more. Then he saw what it was. "Hey, you're locking out your cat," he told Mrs. James.

"Wouldn't own a cat," she told him. She shut the door firmly, and he heard her bolt it from inside.

The gray, blue-eyed cat rubbed against Turner's leg. He stooped to pet it. Very friendly. "Whose little cat are you? Old Blue Eyes," he murmured. "You were there, weren't you? I'll bet you could clear it all up if you just could manage to get the words out, couldn't you?" He rubbed the soft fine hairs behind the cat's delicate ears.

Out on the street, just as he stepped off the curb, a conspicuously anonymous Plymouth turned into Mateo and pulled to a stop in front of 544. Sergeant Herb Greenbaum smiled at him from the passenger seat. The driver looked Turner over, and was plainly bored with what he saw.

Turner was pleased that Greenbaum remembered him. It had been a few years. He had never forgotten the decency and brains with which the L.A.P.D. sergeant had handled the terrified kid Turner had been sent to pick up. Another cop might have tossed the boy in the cooler, sent him up for trial for dealing, but Greenbaum took the time to talk to him, found out why he ran away from Bakersfield, and how he got hold of the stuff he was hawking on the Strip. Greenbaum and Turner had spent most of the night talking to the kid, drinking coffee and eating sandwiches, and Greenbaum had ended up with a pretty good lead to a real dealer. Turner got what he wanted, too—a kid so scared and so grateful he wanted to go home and never sin again. And, he liked to think, a friend. Greenbaum had called to report a major bust a few days later, acting like Turner had as much to do with it as he did.

Turner was really glad to see him. He went up to the car. "How've you been, Sergeant?" he said in a low voice, leaning into the open window. He nodded over at the driver, who gave him a quick nod back and then turned his attention to a ragged thumbnail.

"You moving to L.A., Turner?" Greenbaum asked, friendly enough.

"Thinkin' about it," Turner allowed.

Greenbaum thought about it, too. "Bakersfield's a long commute," he said.

"I'm not with them any more," Turner told him. He went on quickly, heading off questions at the pass. "What brings you down here?" He waved vaguely behind him at the vacant lots and deserted warehouses that lined the block.

"Homicide," Greenbaum answered. "What else?" He peered up at Turner. "The Marshack thing," he added, watching for a reaction.

Turner didn't give him one. "Doesn't ring a bell," he said.

"Oh, no? I'm surprised," Greenbaum said.

"Why is that?" Turner asked genially.

It took Greenbaum a beat or two to decide that his ex-colleague was playing innocent for some reason of his own. He explained, "Well, it made the news. The deceased, Bobby Marshack, had a little something to do with dirty pictures . . . or 'Art,' depending how you feel about naked ladies."

Turner puckered his lips in a tight "O." He waited to hear more.

"The prime suspect is known to us, as they say," Greenbaum told him.

"You guys are good," Turner said.

Greenbaum nodded thoughtfully. "Got a few problems," he said. "The body was moved, and where he *was* killed the place was cleaned up, so there's no weapon, no blood, no signs of violence. I'm talking about the kind of cleaning my wife would go crazy to find somebody to do for *us*." As if it were just an afterthought, he said, "Just a strand of hair, on a pillow. Not Marshack's."

Turner mulled this over. "What color?" he asked. Professional curiosity, one cop to another. He realized of course that Herbie Greenbaum hadn't stopped wondering what he was doing there, even if he hadn't asked. Especially because he hadn't asked.

"Blond," Greenbaum said.

"Real blond?"

"Who knows these days? Also could have come from a wig," Greenbaum said.

"Lab can tell you that," Turner pointed out.

Greenbaum grinned. "You were wasted up there in Bakersfield."

"Aw shucks," Turner said.

"She's still at large." Greenbaum's smile disappeared. He was still scrutinizing Turner's face in his friendliest manner. The driver next to him tapped his abused thumbnail on the steering wheel.

"Who's that?" Turner asked innocently.

"The prime suspect." He looked at Turner coolly and for a long time. "An actual movie star," he went on. "Viveca Van Loren."

Turner shrugged. "Should be easy enough to find."

"She's been quick," Greenbaum said. "But I'm gonna *give* her twenty-four hours, anyway." He watched for a reaction.

"What for?" More professional curiosity.

Greenbaum's eyes narrowed. He squinted up at Turner. "On the outside chance she didn't do it. And that somebody out there *knows* she didn't."

Turner digested this. He and Greenbaum understood each other perfectly. He had done the right thing bringing him in. He put out his right hand to shake. "Nice to see you again, Herb," he said.

Greenbaum nodded. "Same here," he said, meaning it.

Turner went on across the street to his Chevy. He

knew damned well that the reason Greenbaum wasn't getting out of his car immediately was because he was busy putting in a request for a record on one Smith, Turner, ex-cop from the Bakersfield force. He'd be wanting to know if Turner had an L.A. address, and maybe even a reason for being interested in one Van Loren, Viveca.

Or Sternbergen, Alexandra. Turner liked that much, much better.

As he opened the door to the Chevy, he looked back down the street and across to 544. Herb Greenbaum and his driver were just going in. Just before the door closed behind them, the gray cat with the blue eyes darted out into the street. Hit by the sunlight, the cat stopped and looked around, bewildered. Turner left the Chevy door open while he went over to get him. The cat was not only pleased, he seemed grateful to be getting the hell out of there. He purred with his head on Turner's lap all the way home.

She wasn't there, of course. He hadn't really expected her, he guessed, but it amazed him to be so disappointed. There was an empty feeling to the place the minute he walked in; he didn't have to call her or search through the other rooms. But he did. When he came back into the kitchen, the blue-eyed cat was already walking on the formica counter as if he owned the joint. He was rubbing up against the canisters and meowing politely.

"Hungry, huh?" Turner asked him. The cat agreed. Turner went over to him, and it was then he saw her note, printed in marking pencil right on the formica: P.S. YOU'RE OUT OF VODKA.

He petted the cat thoughtfully. He opened a can of salmon that he'd been saving to make a mousse with if he ever felt extravagant. The cat loved the salmon, right out of the can. Why not, at $3.95 a shot . . .

Turner found the Beverly Hills phone book and hauled it up onto the counter next to the cat, who was purring and eating at the same time.

"I'm glad you really appreciate it, because tomorrow it's back to cat food for both of us," he told Old Blue Eyes as he leafed through the pages to find Jacky's Beauty Parlor or Salon or whatever they called them these days.

"It's interesting," Jacky said, letting a soft tendril curl over his finger as he whisked the small hand dryer in careful circles around Alex's head. He studied the new woman in the mirror: short lustrous brown curls framed her face, giving her eyes, her chin and her whole face a new look. She looked younger, too. He turned her chair around so that she could see the final effect for the first time.

"My God," she breathed. "It's Alexandra Sternbergen."

She looked softer, and she was almost glad to see herself.

"But it's not gonna hide you for long, babe," Jacky warned gently.

"No . . . I know." She was reluctant to take her eyes off the way she was, but Alex was nothing if not a realist. "I'm okay for now," she told him. "I've got a place."

Jacky unfolded the towel from her neck and

brushed at some of the brown hairs on the smock that covered her. "Where?"

"A guy's got an apartment," she said, "sort of." A couple of rooms behind a store in a neighborhood even you've never been in, Joaquin. You don't need to know any more, why should I drag you down now that you're on top . . .

Jacky wasn't going to let it go so easily. He was worried about her; she found that touching, truly. "Who?" he asked. "Frankie?"

He was brushing the back of her neck with a talc-touched baby brush. Felt nice, smelled sweet. She bent her head forward and said, muffled into her chest, "No . . . some guy I met by accident." She put her head up and caught his eyes in the mirror. "It's better if you don't know. You keep out of it, Jacky," she said. "You're doing great now, so . . . keep out of this, for your own good, okay?"

Jacky looked sad. He still wanted to help her, protect her, but he'd been trying to do that for ten years and look how much good it had done. Slowly, he gave in to the sense of what she was saying. He nodded at her reflection in his mirror.

She was finished but he didn't want to let her go. There was really nothing more to do to her hair. He was concerned about her situation, sensitive to her precarious emotional state. She knew all that. She couldn't just push off and leave. She swung the chair around to face him without the benefit of mirrors.

"I'll be okay, Jacky," she said.

Jacky shook his head, worried. "I know you're feelin' hurt because . . . y'know. But you can't trust some guy you met in a bar, Alex."

"It was at the airport."

"Whatever. What does he want?"

"What do you mean? Nothing," she told him.

Jacky frowned. "What was he doin' there?"

"Seeing his daughter off."

"How do you know? How do you know he didn't follow you there from that apartment?"

Alex snorted, half-laughing. "No."

"Did you see his kid?" Jacky asked.

"No. But she—"

"Why'd he start talking to you?"

Alex smiled again. "I jumped in his car."

"Which just happened to be right there?"

"He was working on the engine."

"At the airport?"

It did sound a bit strained, all of a sudden. Jacky was smart, street-smart and people-smart. Alex relied on him for that and had for a long, long time. But then she thought about Turner Smith and that goddamned honest friendly face of his, and briefly tossing aside the thought that she might be falling for him, she defended herself.

"He knows I'm innocent," she told Jacky.

"So do I," Jacky said.

"I mean, not because we're friends. He saw there was no body in the shower and then there *was* . . ." She was making a botch of it. Her position was weakening. She had always trusted Jacky so much, why was she fighting him on this one? Was she actually capable of siding with a stranger, a pick-up, against Jacky?

"And then there was," Jacky repeated with exaggerated care.

Alex searched his face. He finished the thought. "He put it there."

"No." But her voice was small and clearly uncertain.

"Who else could have?" Jacky asked rhetorically. "And so easy. You passed out, am I right? It was when I was talking to you on the phone. He was there, wasn't he?"

Hardly able to get the word out, she groaned, ". . . yes."

Taking a guess, Jacky went on, "And didn't he know where Marshack was?"

She felt dizzy. The image of herself from another time whirled for a moment and the lights spun. She gripped the arms of the chair to steady herself. "But *why* would he . . . ?"

The phone rang shrilly, making her jump. Jacky didn't take his eyes from hers as he reached for it.

"What is it, Red . . . For Alexandra Sternbergen . . . ? Who? . . . Turner Smith?" He waited for her reaction, but Alex seemed suddenly frozen, unable to move. "Put him through," Jacky said. He handed Alex the phone.

Chapter Fifteen

THIS NIGHTMARE WAS TAKING QUIRKY TURNS AND NOT doing a thing for her stomach. She stared at the girl she hadn't been in twenty years, wide eyes and all, and was keenly aware of Jacky's concern for her. His dear dark eyes were round and worried. How could she just decide Jacky was wrong and throw in her lot with a one-nighter, a bigoted out-of-work cop from Bakersfield? Was she really that self-destructive? Confused, tentative, she held out her hand for the phone.

"Hello . . ."

"Hello, Alexandra. You okay?"

"Yes . . ."

"I talked to the tenant on the ground floor. She identified your picture, says she saw you come in the building and go upstairs that night."

"What? Who? Who saw me?"

Jacky bit his lip and stared at her anxiously.

"Mrs. James. Tenant in the ground-floor apartment at 544 Mateo. Night before Thanksgiving, remember? She ID'd your photo. Also, I talked with Herb Greenbaum, and—"

Alex cut Turner off. She was confused; too many extras in this flick, too much happening at once. She looked away from Jacky's worried eyes and stared at herself in the mirror, trying to make contact.

"Who?" she interrupted.

"Herbie Greenbaum, you know—Sergeant Greenbaum? L.A.P.D.? You talked to him on the phone? You sure you're all right, you sound druggy or something."

"No. I'm fine," she said, although the panic was rising wildly. Jacky put his hands on her shoulders to calm the trembling. "What'd you talk to . . . Sergeant Greenbaum about—"

"Listen, Alexandra, I had a thought. Maybe it wasn't you, but a double, someone trying to impersonate you. Do you have a wig, like your own hair that maybe you wear when you need to look a certain way and you haven't got time to get it fixed or something? I read that a lot of movie stars do that. If there was a wig, and someone was wearing it . . . you follow?"

It took a minute for the coin to drop. "A wig?" she said finally. She shook her new brown curls. "No. Not for years . . . what do you mean, 'double'? Who'd want to impersonate me?" Now she thought Turner was really crazy.

In the mirror, Jacky frowned.

"Alexandra, I'm coming over there. I'll be there in twenty minutes or so. Wait for me, okay?"

She was near tears. "Don't," she said urgently into the phone, "don't come here!" The line went dead in her ear. "Hello? Turner!" She handed the dead phone to Jacky. He hung it up.

"Alex . . ." he said tentatively, wanting to be kind, "if he's really a friend and he really believes you're innocent, why doesn't he take you in himself? To the police, or at least to a lawyer? That's what I wanted to do."

Alex nodded, her eyes closed, weary beyond belief, unable to think at all.

"Can you tell me why he didn't do that?" Jacky asked her gently.

"No," Alex said. She felt helpless, hopeless. No, she wasn't without help. Here was Jacky, sweet, ever-loving Jacky, her best friend who cared about her, kneeling down next to her now, his big comforting hand over her two cold, quaking fists. "What should I do, Jacky?" she asked him, surrendering all her tough independence at last. "I mean right now," she said. "He's coming here."

Jacky stood up and kissed the top of her head. "Shhhh," he said soothingly. "He won't find you. Come and get comfortable in the studio downstairs. No one will know you're there, you can relax, have a hot tub and a nap, and get your head together. I'll take care of you, okay? Poor baby . . ."

Relief spread its warmth through her like hot marshmallow cocoa after being too long out in a winter storm. Alex got down from the chair and followed him obediently out onto the mezzanine and down the stairs. They crossed the reception area and turned into a wide corridor lined with attractive potted trees that reached up toward the vaulted glass ceiling. Women in variously colored Jacky-smocks sat in comfortable chairs with their feet up, getting themselves blow-dried, color-rinsed, flat-out dyed, curled, straightened, combed and back-combed, brushed, lotioned, manicured, pedicured, waxed, masqued, tweezed, plucked and massaged. A doorway at the end of the corridor led to a private stairway going down. Jacky led the way and unlocked the door to his hideaway apartment. He stepped aside to let Alex go in first; automatically her hand went to the wall switch and the basement room was bathed in a perfect approximation of daylight.

"You know where everything is," he said. Alex nodded. She felt safe here. For a little while. Of course the cops would be here soon; if they were looking for her, they would surely come directly to Jacky. But he would take care of things, and for now she was terribly, terribly tired, too tired to rest. She could come down easy here, with time. There was a deep, inviting couch, a half-kitchen in one corner, a small bar, a Jacuzzi. Cozy, and quiet, and safe. She went over to the bar and began to put together her hangover remedy: Worcestershire, lime, egg. The refrigerator and bar were always well stocked.

"Have a drink with me?" she asked.

Jacky shook his head. "I'm hours behind already."

"They'll wait for you, though," she said.

Jacky agreed with a nod, but he turned to go back to work upstairs. "Will you call Ted Harley?" Alex asked him.

Jacky thought for a minute. Then he shook his head. "We need somebody tougher. Anyway, Ted's not a criminal lawyer." He saw Alex wince at the word. "Sorry, babe. I'll ask around, okay?"

Alex stirred the concoction in her glass with a long spoon. "It's . . . getting late, isn't it?" she said quietly.

Jacky came over and touched her chin with one strong finger. "Won't be until tomorrow," he told her. "You're all right here. And you need some rest."

"I do," she agreed.

Jacky took a vodka bottle from the bar and filled her glass with it. Suddenly, she was pleading. "Can you stay here with me?"

He nodded. "Sure. Sure, babe." But then he remembered, "I've just got to go out to dinner. Okay?"

Alex smiled and nodded weakly. She took a guess: "At the Hardings'?"

"Yes. But an hour and a half, that's all. They go to bed like babies."

Her smile was genuine, affectionate. "Y'look nice," she told him.

Their eyes met only inches apart, and all the old good moments bound them for an instant. Then Jacky turned away. He went over to the Jacuzzi tub. "Want me to turn this on?" he asked.

In another minute they might have had something going, she thought, something nice . . . but they had kept it on the low burner all these years, why turn up the heat now and risk—what? Nothing. Let's stay best pals. "Sure," she told him, and Jacky turned on the swirling motion in the sunken hot tub. Then, as if afraid his life might be passing by and he was going to miss it, he hurried toward the open door leading back upstairs. She stood there, untouched drink in hand, watching his haste to get away from her, wondering did he still love her and did she still love him. But she was too tired to want to think about that or anything else right now.

He stopped at the door. "You'll probably be asleep by the time I get back."

"Wake me up," she told him.

Jacky went on upstairs. Alex took a long slow drink of the hangover concoction and then she went over to the Jacuzzi. As she was taking off her clothes, she heard the sound of doors opening and closing on one of the upper levels. The roiling steaming water seemed absolutely right for her mood . . . how nice if she could just slip down into it and keep on slipping down easily and just melt away . . . but Alexandra Sternbergen wasn't made that way. "Ouch," she muttered as she put her toes into the water.

Upstairs, Jacky checked his private salon, found Alex's scarf on a hook and stuffed it in his pocket for now. He took his keys from another pocket and opened a cabinet. There was nothing in there except a large wig box. He pulled it out by the leather handle. He didn't bother to relock the cabinet.

In the next room, Isabel waited impatiently. She didn't like being left alone, and she hated having to sit here looking at herself in the mirrors that lined the room. Why couldn't she have been born beautiful . . . as well as rich? She sniggered to herself at the thought, but the mirror sniggered back in a very unpleasant way, showing that her expensively straightened teeth still had a slight overbite, and her eyes were too small. Her dark hair hung wet and limp, glued to her head, badly in need of Jacky's touch. Her face was just simply undistinguished. She even had freckles under the makeup. She wondered if Jacky had ever noticed them, and if he loved her in spite of the freckles. Maybe he was the kind who didn't see freckles as a blemish, but something nice, adorable. She crinkled her nose at her reflection but her nose was too wide for girlish gestures and she just looked silly. She needed Jacky to come in here this minute and tell her he loved her. She tried to interest herself in the copy of *Vogue* on her lap, but she couldn't think about anything except what Jacky had to do that was more important than she was. Her eyes kept fixing on the closed door. Any minute he would come through there . . .

And when he did, she leaped from the chair and ran straight into his arms.

"I don't care how long you've been, I know how busy you are, and it's all right, I don't mind waiting for you, darling, honestly I don't—" She kissed him and Jacky kissed her back.

"Isabel . . ."

"Yes, darling."

"Sit down, Isabel."

"Yes, darling. Make me beautiful for the dinner tonight. For you." As she sat down, she saw for the first time what he was carrying. She shrank back from the wig box. "No . . ."

"Just once more," Jacky said.

Isabel shook her head, frightened. "I can't."

"Once more, and then I promise you, we'll be all right."

Sad-eyed, not beautiful to begin with, now Isabel

157

looked like a mournful puppy. He almost expected her to whimper. But she clung to his promise. "*How* will we be all right?" she asked in a small voice.

Jacky was relieved. He could usually get women to do pretty much anything he wanted them to. "You'll see," he said soothingly. For good measure, he put his hands lovingly, caressingly, on her neck and shoulders, the same way he had calmed Alex minutes before.

"How?" Isabel persisted. Her muscles were tense beneath his fingers and he started, ever so gently, to knead them.

"Isabel," he crooned in her ear. "You killed a man. We can't let you stand trial for that, now can we? Of course not. Your life is my life now. We'll do whatever has to be done."

Isabel sought the reflection of his eyes. He felt her neck muscles tighten even more as she whispered, "We ought to tell the police! If I tell them it was an accident . . . how he was hurting me—"

"We can't, Isabel. Maybe we could have right after it happened . . . maybe I was so worried about you I wasn't thinking straight . . . but now . . . it's too late."

"But I didn't mean to do it!"

"I know."

"I was so frightened . . . and angry! I couldn't keep paying for it the rest of my life, a dumb mistake when I was just a kid."

"Shhhh, I know. I know."

She was crying now, big tears that rolled down her cheeks laden with streaks of mascara. "I can't even remember letting him take those pictures. He got me stoned, I was just a kid. And I've been paying for it all these years, and . . . I can't even remember letting him—" She stopped herself, finally, and reached for a tissue from the box on the counter. She blew her nose.

"But he had the pictures," Jacky said.

"Why wouldn't he just take what I could give him and leave me alone? Why did he have to keep asking for more and more and more until . . . and when I said no he hurt me. He was hurting me, Jacky, it was self-defense . . . wouldn't the police believe that?"

"Your father would have to find out, and he'd see the pictures."

Isabel trembled. He soothed her with his hands over her throat and shoulders and her breasts. She turned to him and they kissed. When she caught her breath, she was in control again. "Even if I'd paid off for the negatives, he'd have shown a set of prints to my father, just to get more. That's what you told me and you were right, Jacky. I know you were. God, I couldn't let my father see me . . . that way." She shuddered again.

"Of course not," Jacky said. "We'll be all right. I'm here now, Isabel. We're together . . . we'll get through this together. Now listen, please, very carefully. Someone is on his way here . . ."

Carefully, he began to fit the blond wig, with delicately added dark roots, onto Isabel's head.

Chapter
Sixteen

"Mr. Smith is here to see Alexandra Sternbergen. I told him there was nobody here by that—"

"It's okay, Red. I'll be right down."

Red hung up the phone and smiled at the good-
looking diamond-in-the-rough. There was wit and
sparkle in his eyes. He looked out of place in Jacky's
svelte salon, but most men did. Mr. Smith had a
smile that Red thought was special, and the wild
thing about him was this cat he was carrying.

"What a darling kitty!" she cooed.

Mr. Smith grinned again—really, a terrific smile—
and he put the blue-eyed cat right down on her desk
behind the reception counter. She petted it and it
purred and started walking daintily across the big
appointment book. Red had to laugh and Mr. Smith
did, too.

"He acts like he knows his way around you," he
said.

Red was about to answer him—was it a come-on? when Jacky came down the stairs. He came over but stopped several feet away.

"Can I help you?" he asked, genially.

Turner looked Jacky over. Tough guy, tough enough to be a goddamned hairdresser if he wanted to, and tell anybody who didn't like it to go to hell. Turner figured he could see why a woman would be attracted to him, but personally, the guy made his flesh crawl.

"I'm here to pick up . . . Alexandra," he said, looking Jacky straight in the eye.

Jacky nodded, did some looking of his own, sizing Turner up and down pointedly. "You Turner?"

A bit surprised, Turner nodded. "That's right." Had she been telling her hairdresser-hubby all about him?

"She's upstairs, almost done," Jacky said. "Want to wait?"

Turner seemed to be deciding. He didn't say anything for a minute, then he turned back to the reception desk. He seemed to be looking for something. Suddenly the cat sprang up from behind the desk onto the high counter. He bounded toward Jacky and rubbed against his leg.

"He takes to you, Jacky," Turner commented.

Jacky smiled coldly. "Usually they don't," he said.

There was a brief, quiet moment as both men watched the Siamese arch his back and flatten his ears to move sensuously back and forth against Jacky's $400 jeans. Too bad it wasn't a long-haired cat; it occurred to Turner that whoever had been in the loft closet with the cat would have some hairball to cough up. But Siamese hardly shed at all.

The two men stood watching the cat. The salon was mostly deserted now, with late afternoon shadows darkening the pastel decor and falling across the carpeted floor. The music was off, and the cat's purring was the only sound for a moment or two.

"You always bring your cat everyplace you go?" Jacky asked Turner.

"No, I just picked him up. He sort of followed me. You want him?" Turner countered.

Jacky shrugged. "Why? I look like I got a mouse problem?" He gestured around at the elegant salon.

"No," Turner agreed, not smiling. "But he's a very unusual cat."

Red was listening to the whole exchange with rapt attention. Jacky was not amused, but apparently willing to make conversation until Alexandra came down. "Just a Siamese, no?" he asked.

"This one's seen a lot," Turner told him solemnly.

"How do you tell that?" Jacky asked.

"The eyes," Turner said. He knelt, but the cat slipped away, deeper into the salon, stalking the corners where darkness was settling in.

Red was gathering up her pocketbook and getting ready to leave. "I'll bring in some cream tomorrow," she bubbled happily. She took a lingering look at Turner, but his attention was on Jacky. Red switched off the reception lights and left, with a farewell wink to Turner.

Still kneeling, looking for the cat, Turner looked up just in time to catch sight of Alex hurrying down the stairs from the mezzanine. She was still wearing her scarf over her long blond hair. She was practically running down the steps. She headed for the back door of the salon.

He straightened up quickly. "Alexandra!"

Either she didn't hear him or was deliberately ignoring him. She kept on moving toward the door. Turner started after her, but suddenly Jacky bent down to make a grab at the cat, who darted away. Turner tripped over Jacky and almost lost his balance. He shoved Jacky out of his way and ran after Alex.

The door opened onto an alley, not that it had anything in common with the alley he called home. In Beverly Hills the alleys were not lined with garbage cans, but—if this one was any sample—with exotic trees in antique copper pots instead. Turner almost ran smack into a date palm as he came bursting out of Jacky's delivery entrance. He looked up and down the pristine alley; she was gone. He spotted the nearest parking lot, at the corner, and there she was, just getting into a red BMW 320I.

"Alexandra!" he shouted.

She must have heard him, but she didn't look his way. She started the engine and jack-rabbited out of the lot. In seconds she was into the traffic on Wilshire.

Turner thought about what was going on while he ran, flat-out, around the other side of Jacky's building to the illegal space where he'd left the Chevy. Why was she trying to get away from him? Who the hell's BMW was that? Where was she heading? Why wouldn't she even look at him . . . and as the blood raced through his body from the exercise, the brain cells got all agitated and started percolating. Maybe it wasn't Alex, but somebody who wanted him to think it was—blond hair and a scarf, that was all he'd really seen. If it *was* Alex, he'd catch up with her, find out what was happening.

And if it wasn't Alex—as he forced the stuck door open and rammed himself inside, it seemed more and more likely that it wasn't—then he had to find out who was doubling for her and why.

The summons tied to the wipers got in the way of his vision but he slammed that kicking and bucking Chevy off the curb and into the fast lane of Wilshire boulevard in pursuit of the BMW. He spotted it a couple of blocks ahead, stopped at a long red light, glory be. The street lights came on and the smog lowered slowly over the Hills on his left. Rush hour in L.A.—cars everywhere and going in every direction.

He got more juice out of that old Chevy than he ever had before. He was only trailing by one block when the BMW turned north to Sunset; he stayed with it. East along Sunset toward the canyon roads that run north again toward Mulholland Drive. The traffic thinned as they proceeded; somewhere along the route the woman pulled Alex's scarf from her head, and the pale blond hair flew in the wind, a signal for him to follow.

Turner couldn't possibly know that he himself was being followed. Jacky's Bentley was staying well out of sight—several streets away, in fact—and directing the chase by remote control. Isabel, in the BMW, had one hand gripping the car phone with white knuckles as she steered frantically with the other, following Jacky's directions. She was so scared that tears were rolling down her cheeks and dampening the slightly curled ends of the ash-blond wig. The sun had gone down, but Isabel kept her sunglasses on against the glare of headlights.

"Are you still on Sunset?" Jacky asked her, overcoming his fear of the insecurity of car phones to talk to her through this thing. He would take care of her. She stopped crying.

"Yes."

"Let him stay close. I don't want him to miss you when you turn off."

"Jacky, I'm so scared. I'm not sure I can—"

"*Do* it," Jacky ordered her.

"Th-there's the turnoff," she stammered into the phone. "He's getting closer. I have to slow down to turn . . . what'll I do, Jacky?"

"Do it."

He heard screeching brakes over the phone line, and after a minute, Isabel came back on. "I'm in the canyon, Jacky. He's right behind me."

Jacky checked his watch. "All right. You're doing fine. Now, listen to me. There's a right turn, it's not a cross street, just comes in from the right, about a mile up from where you turned in at Sunset. I forget the name—Iroquois or something like that. You know it?"

"Y-yes, I think so. I'm not sure I can find it in the dark."

"You can find it, Isabel. Darling. I know you can, can't you?"

"Oh, Jacky . . ."

"Come on, Isabel, this is for us. I love you, Isabel."

"I . . . love you, too, Jacky. Oh, I really do."

"When you find that turnoff, remember, it'll be curvy and narrow. You'll do better than he will, so keep it down to 40, 45. Okay?"

"I—there it is." She had to throw the phone down on the seat to grab the wheel with both hands on the sharp turn. She slowed down and picked it up again. "Jacky? I'm on the little road. He just turned off, too."

"Good. Just keep goin' now, up into the hills. And when you get to Mulholland, take a left."

"A left?"

"Yes. A *left*. I'll be there, on Mulholland. I'm comin' a different way. I'll be there first."

"Oh, Jacky . . ."

"Isabel, let him stay close behind, okay? He's not going to catch you, I promise—look what he's drivin'!"

The connection turned into static as Isabel moved deeper into the dark, isolated canyon cut through the rugged hills. Terrified, she watched the rearview mirror more than the winding road before her. Each time it looked like she was about to lose his headlights, she remembered Jacky's instructions and forced herself to slow down. At last she reached the summit of the canyon road where it opened onto Mulholland Drive. You couldn't see any houses up here; all the mansions were nestled behind acres of brush and tall trees and electrified fences disguised as copses of ivy. Usually you made a right turn here, to head on down into the more accessible areas. Isabel turned left. She picked up the phone again.

"Jacky? Can you hear me? Jacky!"

Static. Then his reassuring voice: "You made the left?"

"Yes. I'm on Mulholland. It's scary up here—no more houses and the road is full of ruts . . ."

"How far behind is he?"

"Where are you, Jacky?"

"I'm here, I'm here, don't worry. It's all going fine, Isabel. Trust me, okay?"

"Okay. But I'm so scared . . ."

"Isabel, listen now, this is important. There's a bad stretch of road coming up on Mulholland, you know it, don't you? It's the place you hate to drive . . ."

"That's right." Her fingers were clutching the wheel and the phone so hard that her nails were cutting little bloody half-moons into her palms.

"Right, okay," Jacky said calmly. "Now, somethin's gonna happen. You'll hear brakes, or skidding, or maybe worse. It doesn't matter." He said the last three words in a deliberately final, emphatic voice, the voice of authority. It helped her. "All I want you to do is drive another hundred yards after that, after you hear the sounds—and then pull over. Just off the road, where it's safe. And wait. Just wait. Don't do anything, don't get out of the car. Wait. I'll come for you."

Driving up toward the dangerous stretch, Isabel just nodded. She couldn't say anything. She just nodded and clutched the wheel and watched the old Chevy sending out fumes and gamely keeping up with her in the rearview mirror.

"Are you all right?" Jacky asked.

Isabel nodded again. She tried but nothing came

out. She tried again, with her throat and mouth so dry no words would come. "Uh-huh," she managed to whisper into the phone.

"Good girl. I'm waitin' at the bend. Just do as I say and everything will be all right. Okay?"

But she had come to the crest of the ridge. Both hands were on the wheel and her eyes glued onto the incredible drop at the edge of the road. High above the city, the ridge was like a landing strip in the sky. Below hung all the lights of western Los Angeles, Beverly Hills, Bel Air and Westwood, and even more distant, Santa Monica and the ocean, whose black expanse merged with the sky. There was no fence or railing or marker along the rim of the road, just a sudden dropping away into nothingness.

The BMW came cautiously around the dangerous curve, passing the parked Bentley. Isabel kept her eyes straight ahead, on the road. The Bentley engine revved up, then Jacky shifted into low. Kicking up gravel, the Bentley surged halfway across Mulholland just as Turner's Chevy came careening along the bend. The Bentley smashed up against the Chevy, broadside.

The Chevy's hood sprang up. The passenger door was crunched with a sickening sound. The other door popped open, the trunk lid flew open and slammed shut . . . and the Chevy was driven sideways across its lane, off Mulholland and out into blackness. It tumbled down the ravine, end over end, and burst into flame, lighting up the night.

Chapter
Seventeen

THE BENTLEY ROLLED CAUTIOUSLY TO THE BROKEN edge of the road. The flaming wreckage of the Chevy lit the darkness far below where it had come to its final stop. Here and there along the steep ravine small brush fires flared where the car had touched as it careened end over end. The little fires gave no light and were already dying out, darkening the night even more completely. There were no stars. There was only the fiery mess down there, so far away it already seemed remote, having nothing to do with this high clean place. Jacky backed the Bentley and turned back onto the Drive. He slowed and stopped where the BMW was parked, where the road widened slightly under an overhanging rock. As he stepped out of his car, Isabel started to open her door. She would have run to him, needing comfort.

"Stay in the car," Jacky ordered her. He slid in alongside her.

"What—?" Isabel gasped. She was having trouble getting enough air into her lungs; her whole body was shaking visibly. There was no time. Another car might come by any minute; if they were seen it could get very ugly. As gently as possible, crooning to soothe her, Jacky took the wig from her head.

"You go home now, sweetheart," he said.

"You're supposed to be there," she told him. She seemed dazed, out of it.

"I will," Jacky promised.

"At seven thirty sharp, Daddy said."

"I'll be there at seven thirty," he assured her softly.

Isabel looked at him with huge, frightened eyes. Her lower lip was trembling, on the verge of sobs. "I want them to like you," she said insistently. But she was looking at him as if she wasn't really sure who he was.

"They will," Jacky assured her. He put his hand over her cold limp fingers. "Can you drive?" he asked.

Isabel just stared at him, not answering. Jacky reached over and turned the key. The engine started up and idled quietly. "It's all over, Isabel," Jacky told her. "Nothing more to worry about, ever. Just drive home now and I'll be there at seven thirty promptly. All right?"

He got out of the BMW and shut the door quietly. He came around in the darkness to her side and leaned in to pull on the lights. He kissed her forehead. She still hadn't said anything, but she put the car in gear. Jacky stepped back and watched the BMW disappear into the darkness.

A car rushed past him.

Now the darkness was absolute. Jacky got into the Bentley and coasted down the canyon drive for a few hundred yards before turning on his headlights. Then he headed for the glitzy glow of civilization far below.

A Jacuzzi is a wonderful thing. For a little while you can just pretend to be a blob of nature, not responsible for what you do or what will become of you. You float there, while muscle tensions melt like chocolate bits in a big sweet cookie. But it doesn't last; after a while your skin puckers and your heart thinks it might start pounding from the hot swirling waters and it's time to climb out and act human again. Alex wrapped herself in Jacky's dark blue terrycloth robe, enjoying its hugeness around her. She picked up the glass of vodka she had poured, looked at it long and hard, and then set it down. She went over to the couch to curl up and wait for him; maybe she could sleep now. The hot pulsing water had made her drowsy. Jacky always had the cure for everything.

She slept. In her sleep she was trying to find the exit—no, the entrance; she was walking backwards through a maze and trying to figure out how she'd gotten into it. She was alone, terribly alone . . . except that there was a slow and horrible prickly feeling that she was *not* alone at all. Someone was watching her and laughing silently at her predicament, someone very close, so close she could feel his cool breath on her cheek. She screamed and lunged away from him, almost knocking herself off the couch onto the floor.

Her scream still echoing in her ears, Alex saw what had frightened her so—the blue-eyed cat had leaped from the couch and was standing his ground on the rug, staring back at her. He must have been breathing in her face, staring at her and entering her dream—but where the hell did he come from? It was the same blue-eyed Siamese she had awakened with before, in another place. *What the hell was he doing here? What was going on . . . ?*

Slowly, Alex got to her feet. Her heart was beating rapidly, but not from the hot water—that had been hours ago. From fear. She tried to calm herself, but her drink was on the bar across the room and there was only herself and the cat. He stood his ground, watching her, and then he deliberately turned his back on her and headed slowly for the door. His tail was straight up in the air: follow me.

Hypnotized, and shaking with terror, Alex followed. Up the stairs, to the main salon. Usually it was bright and filled with people, a busy place with daytime energy; it was a strange and eerie place now, empty and dark with shadows lurking and someone waiting there for her. She knew someone was there. *There!* a sound—from the mezzanine over her head. She looked up sharply: nothing but shadows, stillness, an ominous sense of—something.

She made her way to the stairs and took a single step up. Someone was on the mezzanine. She raised her head to look up. In the shadows, she saw two eyes staring back at her, glaring from a hard inner light, unblinking, clear-sighted. Blue eyes. It was the cat. He was waiting for her to follow. She took another step; her bare foot missed the riser and she almost tripped. She grabbed the handrail. Her sudden movement startled the cat and his eyes disappeared. She thought of the Cheshire Cat in *Alice in Wonderland*—only the smile remained. Alex huddled deeper into Jacky's enormous robe, and she climbed another stair.

With each step, another question drove a stake of doubt through her: Could she be hallucinating (it had happened before, just before she had gone to that place in Baja to dry out), was it really a cat she saw, was it the same cat—or had there been a cat at all on Mateo Street? She might have hallucinated them both . . . or someone might be trying to drive her crazy.

She was at the top of the winding half-stairway. It was almost impossible to see anything, but— something moved. The curtain across the storage closet at the top of the stairs had fluttered—or had she imagined it? She moved slowly toward it, feeling her way along the wall in the dark. She thought of the closet in the Mateo Street loft; someone had been lurking there. A profound sense of having performed this exact act before came over her—a *déjà vu* so powerful she thought she knew what she would find when she opened the curtain. This time he might kill her . . . this time, it might be too late to turn and run away . . . don't open that curtain, Alexandra, are you crazy . . .

She yanked it aside. The eyes . . . it was the cat, and he was real. She knelt down in the darkness and stroked his soft clean fur. The cat was trembling as much as she was. She lifted his chin and stared into his blue eyes, which were, she could see now, terrified.

"I know how you feel, kid," she whispered. Then, clearing her throat, she tried to speak at a normal level. "You have a brother lives downtown? Huh? Say, how did you get here, oh, God, please tell me . . ."

She had completely unnerved herself. She stood and looked around, but it was too dark to see anything. The cat rubbed against her legs for company and comfort. Alex felt along the wall for the light switch, found it and flicked it on. It illuminated the storage area beyond the curtain: rows of shelves lined with wigs on stands. Under each wig was neatly printed the name of a customer. The cat slipped away and Alex turned to follow him. Suddenly, something registered in her mind: click. Slowly, she turned back to the storage closet.

VIVECA VAN LOREN. Her name under a wig stand; her blond wig from the movie days. She'd seen it a hundred times, but something was different. Something was off. For a minute, she didn't know what, and then she saw it—a small, open jar of black Meltonian Shoe Cream on the shelf next to her wig.

In a terrible rush, she understood. Fear stiffened her fingers as she took the wig off the stand and examined its dark roots. The hair hanging limply from her hand, she examined her fingers, stained with the black polish. She couldn't even pet the cat for fear of tainting him with the horrible, sticky, incriminating stuff.

* * *

"We'll take our coffee in the living room," Mrs. Harding told the butler. She rose to leave the table.

Jacky's first dinner with Isabel's family seemed to go well. He put his charm into automatic and it worked despite his distractions; he was concerned about Isabel, who was visibly on edge. He hoped that it was only a natural concern for the impression he was making on her parents. But he thought it wise to get her the hell out of there as soon as possible. Besides, there was unfinished business.

"I won't have any coffee, thank you, Mrs. Harding," he told Isabel's mother, rising to his feet. "In fact, I'm going to do something terribly rude. I've got to take Isabel away from you this minute."

Isabel was startled. "Jacky—" she began, but he cut her off.

"Trust me, darling." He turned to her mother again and with an air of genial conspiracy, he said, "I'm sworn to secrecy, but fifty people are waiting to shout 'Surprise!' "

Mrs. Harding loved it. "I understand. Run along, my dears. It was lovely meeting you, Mr. Manero."

"Dinner was wonderful," Jacky said sincerely. He held her hand for a moment in almost an old-world gesture. Then he turned and shook hands with Mr. Harding. "Until next time," he said.

He ushered a confused Isabel out into the hall. She whispered to him furiously. "Are you crazy? Did you see Daddy's face? You were rude—"

The butler was standing at the doors to the dining room, waiting. "Fred," Jacky told him, "would you bring Miss Harding's car around?" Fred nodded and went down the hall toward the rear of the house.

Isabel was on her own turf, and put her foot down.

"I'm not taking another step until you explain this extraordinary behavior," she told him, with something nastily like a pout.

Jacky took her arm. "It's Alex," he whispered.

She stared at him, not comprehending, and then, horrified, she did comprehend. Her hand flew to her mouth. "No . . . Jacky, no . . ."

"When Turner called her, he told her about the double," Jacky explained patiently. "We can't let the police hear that, can we? It'll be easy, darling. She's drunk and passed out by now."

"I can't . . . " Isabel protested. She was near the edge. She was in her own home, and wanted to stay where it was safe. But Jacky was shaking her; he was strong and smart and he loved her . . . she had to do what he said, but she couldn't. "I can't," she repeated weakly.

"It has to be done," he told her. "And *now*."

Isabel whimpered softly. But she went along with him to the front door and leaned against him as he held it for her and then she walked out to her BMW and let Fred open the passenger door for her. She got inside and let Jacky drive to the place where she would have to kill someone again. She knew now it would never end.

Chapter
Eighteen

ALEX HAD POURED A FULL GLASS OF VODKA FOR
herself, but it sat on the coffee table untouched. She
just didn't want to dull the sharp edge of her anger.
She wanted to stay alert, and stay angry, to confront
him soberly when he came back. The hurt little girl
who had been betrayed by her best friend gave way
slowly to the fury of a woman scorned. She thought
of a thousand and one forms of revenge, most of
them a credit to the Marquis de Sade.

She paced the cozy studio apartment, touching
things. A paperweight she had given him one Christ-
mas, not too long ago. A book she'd lent him years
ago, a set of bar tools for mixing fancy drinks. She
stood looking down at the big white couch, remembering making love, not so very long ago. She had
trusted him completely, the only man she had
trusted since her father. Hah. They had both turned
out to be rats.

Thinking about her father brought tears to Alexandra's eyes, so she'd damn well better stop thinking about him if she really wanted to stay away from that nice tall vodka. Anyway, he was a whole lot less of a rat than both the husbands she had picked—*he* only walked out. He hadn't tried to pin murder on her. She could really start feeling sorry for herself, except that wasn't her style. To hell with all of them, and you, too, Turner Smith.

Now she was truly on her own. Keep sober and use the old noodle, she told herself. You used to be kind of bright. She made a fire the way she'd been taught in the Campfire Girls, and when it was cracking and blazing, she sat on the floor staring into the flames and thinking. Then she picked up the phone and dialed.

"Sergeant Greenbaum."

"Hello, Herbie. This is Viveca."

"Miss Van Loren? I'm glad to hear from you." He paused. "I have some news . . ."

And then he told her, and when they had hung up, Alex put her head down on a pillow she had needle-pointed for Jacky a long time ago, and she wept.

She thought she heard the sound of a car on the gravel driveway overhead, but it stopped and no one came into the building. Alex got up and opened the studio door so she could hear when Jacky arrived. She didn't have too long to wait. She heard the Bentley swing in, the door slam, and then the footsteps overhead. She picked up the wig and stood in the middle of the room, holding it, waiting for him to come downstairs.

* * *

From the look on his face, he had obviously expected to find her drunk and passed out, dead to the world. And he had Isabel Harding with him, walking behind like a dutiful dodo, looking scared. What did she have to be scared of? She'd have a few good years before Jacky turned on her. But Alex didn't want to look at her; she wanted to look long and deep into Jacky's eyes and try to understand how she had misjudged him so fatally all these years.

"What did you do?" she asked him coldly.

Jacky didn't answer. Behind him, Isabel was chalk-white and quiet.

"What did you *do?*" Alex repeated. She looked at Isabel and then back at Jacky, speaking only to him. "Or did *she* do it? You killed that guy Marshack, didn't you? Jacky?"

He just stood and watched her, his mind racing almost visibly. In vain, Alex searched for one last residual sign of caring in his face. "Did you kill him, Jacky . . . or did that skinny little inbred broad do it?"

He still didn't answer. She stared at him, unable to believe what she knew was true. "You set me up . . . ?" She shook the wig and held it at arm's length. "With this? Why, Jacky? For her? For that?"

Jacky was clearly unhappy to see her waving the wig around, but still he said nothing. He was thoughtful, but he was a stone wall. Behind him, Isabel Harding reached out a hand to clutch his sleeve. Alex ignored her, seeing only Jacky.

"Christ, wasn't I anything to you?" she asked sadly. "Am I blind?" Her anguish deepened. She was beyond tears. "I can see that you wanted in . . . I could see that, Jacky. I could understand it. But . . . not by having me put away or gassed to get there! No, Jacky."

He looked away from her eyes, down at the wig she still held. "How did I miss it?" she asked. "We were so close, so long . . . why didn't I see . . . what you were capable of? What you could do to me? You must have had it in you, why didn't I see that?"

It was a monologue, but she didn't care whether he was listening or not—whether the two of them were listening. She was talking for herself, sorting things out, talking her way out of shock, trying to understand, thinking maybe if she could understand, she would know where to go, what to do.

"Turner knew. He tried to tell me. He said to me, 'Don't you want to know what's going on?' . . . I guess I didn't. Well . . . I do now. You look scared, Isabel. That's your name, isn't it, Isabel Harding? I've heard of you. What are you so scared of? That maybe someday he'll do the same to you? Maybe. I wish somebody had clued me in ten years ago. Jesus, Jacky—ten years. You must be in real trouble to . . . yeah, I guess you got in big trouble and I was—what the hell, not doing much of anything anyway, right?"

No answer. "That's right. You didn't set me up, Jacky. I did," she said, seeing clearly for the first time in a very long, long while.

"You're drunk," Jacky said.

"I'll bet you wish I was, Jacky," she answered. There was something ugly about the way the two of them were staring at her. Suppose they came here expecting to find her passed out . . . then what?

What would have been different, if she had gone the way they planned for her to?

It occurred to her that she was in danger.

"I called the cops," she said.

Jacky took a giant step toward her and grabbed the wig out of her hands. With one quick motion, he threw it in the fire. The rancid stench of burning hair rose with the quickened flames.

He turned back to her. "You can't prove any of it," he said.

"Turner can," Alex said.

"Turner?"

Alex nodded. "He knows about the wig, the double—making a scene on Mateo Street that night so the neighbors would peg me."

Jacky took a step toward her. "Turner's dead, Alex," he told her harshly.

He reached out for her arm, but she shrugged him off, standing her ground. "He's alive," she countered.

Jacky shook his head and kept moving toward her.

"He's alive!" Alex shouted at him, trying to hold him off with a buckshot spray of words. "That car of his . . . the door popped open . . . he fell out before the car went over . . ."

Jacky stopped and stared at her. Was she bluffing? How did she know—

They were all startled by a sudden loud rapping at the main door of the salon. It seemed to release Isabel from her spell, and she turned without a second's hesitation to run up the stairs. Jacky stood there for a moment, staring at Alex, trying to figure it. Then he, too, turned and ran up to the reception area. Alex kept a respectable distance between them and herself as she went up.

Police car lights were flashing and blinking wildly in the dark night beyond the open doorway. They cast a weird and lively dance across the room. As Alex came up, she saw Isabel talking with a young man in jeans and a Rams T-shirt. Greenbaum, she guessed. Good, sweet, dear old Herbie Greenbaum, thank God. She came close enough to hear what Isabel Harding was telling him.

"—terribly jealous, he's . . . Latin, you know, it's the only way that I can explain what he did . . ."

Jacky heard it, too. It was the start of something he wasn't going to be able to handle. "NO!!!" he yelled, going for Greenbaum. Two uniformed cops stopped him from getting too close.

"Poor baby," Alex murmured.

The cops hustled him out of there and after a minute or so, Greenbaum turned Isabel Harding over to someone else and turned to Alex.

"Miss Van Loren?" he asked politely, unnecessarily.

"Herbie Greenbaum, right?" she asked, also unnecessarily.

"This is a real honor, meeting you," he said.

"I think the pleasure's on my side this time, Herbie," she told him. "How's Turner? Any news?"

"Still critical. No change since I talked to you. C'mon, I'll take you over there if you want to go."

"Let's go," she said.

St. Vincent's Hospital was wrapped in the silence of midnight except in the Intensive Care Unit. The green lights on Turner's life-support machines were bopping up and down and making all kinds of beeps and cackles. She stood there and watched his chest move up and down, unaware that her own breathing was pacing his, trying to breathe for him, willing him to do it on his own. She stayed there for a long time, until finally a nurse asked her to leave.

Greenbaum was waiting outside the ICU. Not smoking, not reading, not drinking coffee—pure waiting. He looked up as she came out, a question on his face. She smiled and showed with her fingers how the oscilloscope was counting off Turner's heartbeats and brainwaves and all.

"Still alive," she said.

Greenbaum nodded. He stood up. "What can I do for you?" he asked.

"Nothing. Thank you," she added wearily, gratefully.

Greenbaum stuck his hand in his pocket and came up with a set of keys. He handed them to her. She looked at them, then at him. The significance of the gesture escaped her, although the keys looked vaguely familiar. Too tired for games, Greenbaum, her look said, so tell me.

"It was impounded. That '63 Mercedes you left at the airport."

"Oh. Yeah." A thousand years ago, part of a barely remembered other life.

But Greenbaum was pleased with himself and wanted her to be pleased, too. "I got it released, had them leave it downstairs," he told her.

Alex smiled wanly. "Thanks, Herbie."

Herbie nodded. "L.A.'s hell without a car," he said.

"I love you, Herbie," she said.

"I love you too, Miss Van Loren."

There was nothing to do but go home. They walked down the long quiet corridor together, then down the elevator and out to the street. Her car was there as promised, looking a bit uncomfortable in the company of an unmarked police car. Greenbaum walked her over to the Mercedes and waited while she slid herself behind the wheel. He waved and went on over to where his driver was waiting. Alex headed for home. She had never felt so lonely in her life.

Chapter
Nineteen

SOME HOME. HAD ANYBODY—HAD SHE—EVER DONE any living here? It was about as homey as a motel room. She looked around at her unfinished attempts at decorating the place. She went into the bedroom, dropped Frankie's clothes on the chair and took a long hot shower. It took a minute for her to stand firmly on the shower's tiles—the memory of Marshak's body so recently slumped there was still vivid. After toweling off, she tried on a couple of things before she was satisfied with a soft lavender print dress. She brushed her hair and decided she would let it grow out to its natural color, hoping that it would turn out as well as Jacky had done it. She liked the way she looked, for the first time in a long time.

She went into the living room, sat down, almost immediately got up again. She went to the kitchen and opened the refrigerator. She threw the tacos down the pig and ground them up with cold water roaring full-force until there was nothing left but air. She looked in the fridge again—a whole lot of wine, all right. Fuck it. She slammed the door shut.

She picked up the phone and tried the number again. Still busy.

She glanced over at the bar. It would help her to grab a little sleep; just one drink would relax her enough to catch an hour or two's rest, God knew she needed a rest. But she didn't go for it. She turned on the television.

One of those late-night zombies with too much energy. She watched him without sound for a minute, then turned the dial past religious zealots, topless hookers being interviewed, reruns of a 1950's quiz show, and a lot of color patterns indicating that the stations were off the air. It was two in the morning. A long night coming up; she thought about the vodka bottle sitting there waiting to soothe her nerves. What was so bad about drinking a little vodka in the middle of the night when you needed it, she asked herself, and didn't bother to answer.

She went into the bedroom to pick up a book she had been meaning to read for weeks. The novel had gotten good reviews, sounded interesting, and was being considered for a film. Someone had said the lead was absolutely perfect for her. When the director called, she would be ready if she'd read the book. She had started it a few times, curled up in a chair with the book and a glass of wine; somehow she had always finished the wine and never the book.

It was good, and yet she couldn't concentrate. She kept seeing blips of an oscilloscope between her eyes and the words on the page. Every now and then she tried the phone again, but the line stayed busy. Probably out of order, and nobody knew it. Fine thing for a hospital.

When she got hungry, she went out again, to the closest all-night hamburger stand, and brought the greasy bag home with her. She ate the hamburger and drank the Tab and kept it down. She wished she had bought some cookies. She tried the number again and this time she got through. No change in Turner's condition. Now it was 3:50.

The weather channel said that sunrise would be at 6:42. At 5:38 she left the apartment, got back in the Mercedes and drove toward downtown L.A.

The bars opened early in that part of town. She felt more than a little shaky, but she drove on past them. She parked near a little lake and watched it until the water began reflecting gray rays of daylight to compete with the cold yellow streetlamps shimmering down. Then she sat some more, waiting for it to be late enough for normal people to be up. Then she couldn't wait any longer, and drove over to the hospital.

The reception area was a bit chaotic, people waiting for visiting hours to begin. You were supposed to have a pass. She stole one from a nurse's desk when the woman wasn't looking. She pushed by the duty guard along with a family of non-English-speaking Pakistanis. In the elevator, she listened carefully to the P.A. system as it paged Dr. Brinker, Dr. Hauser and someone named Emilio Cortezar who was wanted in the maintenance shop at once.

She got off the elevator and went purposefully toward the nurses' station. "Dr. Hauser phoned me to meet him in the I.C.U.," she said brusquely, moving straight on through the closed doors with the little glass windows. She went to Turner's bed. It had been stripped. The mattress was folded over.

Alex whirled in panic to find the duty nurse. "Where is he, what happened, is he—"

"Who?" She was bored, had heard it all before.

"Turner Smith," she said in a low voice. *She's going to say he died. I don't know whether I can stand that.*

"He's been moved to—let me see—room four-six-two."

"He's—all right?"

The nurse looked at her disapprovingly. "He's a very sick man," she said sternly.

"But not critical!" Alex almost shouted.

"Guarded."

"Thanks," she said from the bottom of her heart. She hurried out and down the corridor until she found the room. She opened the door and went in.

He looked very weak, beat up and still hitched to a lot of monitors and IV's, but some of his human color was back and he was breathing. His eyes were closed. She knew she might not have much time before they booted her out, so she didn't waste any of it.

"Wake up, Turner. Hey, Turner?"

His eyes opened. He was thinking that she looked familiar, but not entirely. At first she thought his mind had been affected, but then she realized that he had never seen her hair this color and cut this way. And he was still very weak.

"Who the hell're you?" he managed.

Alex grinned. "That sports announcer you liked from Cincinnati," she told him.

"Never liked him," Turner said. It was an effort for him to talk. It hurt. "How'd you get in here?"

"Dr. Hauser said it was okay," she said.

"Doctor's name is Pitkin."

"I use Hauser," she told him.

He nodded against the pillow. He liked the way she looked, she could tell. "I never trusted Manero," he said weakly, "but I sure love how he made you look."

Alex leaned closer to confide in him. "He didn't do it. I always used to look this way."

Turner sighed. "I should have known you then," he said.

"Yeah, you should have," she agreed.

Turner lay there, aching and turning things over in his mind. "Where is he?" he asked after a minute. "Jacky?" He winced with pain. His jaw was wired and some interesting colors were rising on his cheek and forehead.

"With your pal Herbie."

"They got enough on him?" he wanted to know.

"I'm not sure," Alex told him. "Miss Harding says he did it but he says she did."

Turner flinched with pain when he smiled. "Bye-bye, Jacky," he said.

"What d'you mean?"

Turner squinted a badly bruised eye at her. "Who do you think they'll believe? Her? Or a sp—Joaquin Manero?"

"Who do you believe?" Alex asked him levelly.

There was a long look between them, and then Turner nodded. "I think she did it," he said. "I think

189

they'll send him away. I think she'll do a little time or none. I think it's the way it is . . . and it's a bitch."

Alex nodded thoughtfully but she didn't say anything.

"Some water, please?" Turner asked her.

She poured some out of a tin pitcher into a paper cup, held it for him with a bent plastic straw while he drank.

"What're you going to do?" he asked her.

"When?"

"Y'know."

She shrugged. "I don't know yet. Work. Wait for you to get sprung . . ."

"That's a nice thought," Turner said. "But . . . all we know about each other is a day and a half on the run, somebody tryin' to kill us."

"Brings people together," she said. "Maybe that's as good a way as there is to start. The rest'll be like Sunday on the farm." She was kind of pleading with him, but it was important enough so that she didn't care.

"What do you know about a farm?" he groaned. "But . . . I have great hopes for you, Alexandra."

She heard what he was saying. "What about for us?" she persisted.

He didn't answer, just looked at her sadly. She knew. "You don't want to live with a lush, is that it?" she said.

He realized what it took for her to call herself that, to make the admission. He admired it, but . . . she was right. "Would you want to?" he asked.

"It's been a couple of days. And a night. With no help," she told him, the words coming hard. She knew it wasn't much, except to her.

He gave her a long, fond look. Really fond, she thought. But he didn't say anything.

Alex said, "We say goodbye, then?"

He nodded, breaking her heart.

"Whatever makes you happy," she said.

Suddenly, the door opened and a nurse walked into the room. She gaped at Alex.

"You been here all night?" she accused.

"Yes," Alex lied. "Just leaving."

The nurse opened the drapes to the sun. She shoved a thermometer into Turner's mouth, checked the IV drip and left the room. Alex stood there.

He said something around the thermometer; maybe it was "Take good care" or something close to it.

"Sure . . . whatever you said," Alex agreed. She went to the door.

Turner took the thing out of his mouth. "You've got a right to know something," he said.

"A right?"

"Yeah."

She waited. Then he said, "I was a drunk for ten years. I got cut but . . . I'd been on the way out a long time."

Neither of them said anything—but the words stayed on the air between them like a gift he had given her. Something he found it hard to part with, but wanted her to have.

"You came back," she said quietly.

He barely nodded. "Tryin' to."

"It can be done," she said. It was almost a question.

Turner was worn out and in pain, and she should have left him in peace. But because she couldn't seem to open the door, he tried to help her out.

"I know this trick: I count to three . . . you disappear," he said almost in a whisper.

She stood there, taking it.

"One . . . thanks for visiting."

"You're welcome."

"Two . . . was a pleasure meeting you, Alexandra."

"Yes. It was."

"Three . . . good luck."

"You, too."

She opened the door and went out. It closed behind her.

Turner, exhausted, spent, turned to the green blips monitoring his life signs on the television screen. He couldn't see it clearly because his eyes were filled with tears.

"Didn't work," Alex said.

He looked up gravely. "Never did see that damn trick done right," he said.

"You never will," she told him.

He could hardly talk. But . . . "Whatever makes you happy," he managed to say.

"You," Alex told him. "You make me happy."

When she bent over to kiss him, his green blips took a very strong surge in the right direction.